PRAISE FOR
SCOTT A. LERNER

THE WICCAN WITCH OF THE MIDWEST

"I am impressed with how Scott was able to tell such a great story in such a short amount of time…. This would make my list of books to read during Halloween. It had quite an interesting twist. I was hooked from the very first page."
—Fic Gal

THE FRATERNITY OF THE SOUL EATER

"An exceptionally entertaining read…. A master of the genre, Scott Lerner's latest novel continues to document his originality and skill as a storyteller…. Highly recommended for both personal reading lists and community library collections."
—John Burroughs for the Midwest Book Review

"Not only is this an interesting plot full of twists and turns, but Lerner's characters, Sam and Bob, are witty and endearing. The book is not just plot-heavy, as many genre books can be. This supernatural thriller is full of characterization, which is perfect for fans of the series who already love Sam Roberts and also for new readers who will like him immediately and want to go back and read the first two installments."
—Margo L. Dill, The News-Gazette

"A quick and very amusing read. Even when they are getting whooped on Sam and his friend Bob, have a weird sense of humor, that just won't let them stop making smart remarks…. This book isn't just funny, it has some mystery, and a bit of horror, and even some adventure. It is a standalone book, but you will probably want to read the other books in the series too, if you haven't already. I liked the last book, and this one was just as good. Maybe even better."
—Simple Wyrdings

"Lerner gives us characters that are full of fun, bluster and charm, yet have that energy that you feel is trustworthy. His dynamics between his characters and protagonists are both strange and unlikely, but at the same time intriguing and interesting. You find yourself immersed in a story that takes you to the edge of darkness, twisting and realigning your own take on life…. A fun and unique find."
—Tic Toc Reviews

"Another fun round with Sam and Bob…. Bob always has a way of making light of whatever happens. Whether he shoots a cobra or sees a desiccated corpse, he finds humor in it. I like Bob. He reminds me of Shaggy from Scooby-Doo, right down to the van with purple shag carpet and the hash brownies."
—Romancing the Book

Five Stars: "A unique and creative plot. Sam himself is a likeable character—he's smart, and his close relationships with Bob and Susan help bring him alive on the page; but as a reader you also feel how conflicted he is about the things he's recently learned walk in the world."
—E. Lucas, top-rated Amazon Reviewer

"The pace of the story is fast, so you're turning pages as fast as your eyes will allow…. My favorite character is Sam's friend Bob. Everyone has or needs a Bob in their life. He's there for his friend. He's handy with a computer and good to bounce ideas off. I don't want to give any spoilers but the story is a thriller mystery. It's fun, interesting, and good."
—The One True Faith Blog

"A suspenseful thriller that grabs you right from the start, it takes you into an ancient world of long held secrets and grotesque murders. A true page turner."
—Tribute Books Mama

RULER OF DEMONS

"There are exciting twists in the fast-paced plot that raise the

stakes for our heroes. *Ruler of Demons* doesn't feel like a horror story, but there's strong tension and entertaining banter throughout the book. It's the only novel about demons, mutilation, and the apocalypse that can potentially leave a smile on the reader's face."
—Brian Bandell for the New York *Journal of Books*

"A FUN book! The main character has a really cool sense of humor (even if he is a lawyer) and even when he is about to get killed he doesn't completely lose it. The book does have its dark side but on the whole it is the sort of book you should read when the weather is bad and you need cheering up ….The mystery part of the story was really well done too. You really don't know right up till the end exactly how it will go. Every time I thought I had it figured out…some other thing got thrown in to shake things up."
—Simple Wyrdings Blog

"*Ruler of Demons* is creepy and fast-paced, with a few thrilling twists to keep the reader up at night. It's also sprinkled with the kind of humor one hears in a police procedural show, the wisecracks one imagines veteran cops make. They may not be the most realistic bits of dialogue, but the blurb on the back cover gives a good idea of the wild-ride tone of the novel: 'Only eleven shopping days till Christmas. And less than a week to save the world.'"
—Paige Fumo Fox for Chicago *Book Review*

"The novel is jam-packed with details from TV and movie references to mouth-watering descriptions of local cuisine. Lerner has a keen eye for the world his characters inhabit making it come alive for the reader in all three dimensions."
—Carol Robart, The Plot Thickens Blog

"*Ruler of Demons* is well written, with plenty of humor and plenty of adventure and Lerner's cast of characters are intriguing and intelligent. Readers who like a bit of weirdness and darkness in their reading (kind of like my oldest son!) will adore this."
—Sharon's Garden of Book Reviews

"One of the best techniques in this thriller is the pace. Your

heart will race. But you won't have a heart attack, because the author is skilled in breaking up the pace with humor. Sam's and Bob's banter will make you laugh. Sometimes you have to stop and think, and then you'll guffaw…. They're clever, witty, and likeable. I think everyone will enjoy this story. You won't figure it out. You won't expect any of the twists the characters find themselves going through. You won't want the world to end."
—The One True Faith Blog

"Sam's belief in logic and living in the now directly opposes the nature of the crimes he's trying to solve, giving the book an added sense of tension as the reader is forced to look at things from the outside in…. *Ruler Of Demons* might not be bursting with peace on earth and yuletide cheer, but for the murder mystery fan who gravitates toward the macabre, it makes the perfect stocking stuffer."
—Tribute Books

"Sam's a fun character who inhabits a world full of them. Their interactions are natural and entertaining and the tension builds nicely as the book progresses. I found myself anxious to see how it all turned out and ended up reading it in a day. I recommend this for anyone who likes a good mystery with religious overtones."
—Jamie White's Culture Shock Blog

"What pulled me in about this novel were the characters. Sam and Bob have a great friendship. I loved how Bob always started about food, and how Sam managed to stay calm, no matter what. Their inside jokes made me feel connected to them. Sam was a bit of an average Joe, which made him all the more intriguing when he's thrown in the world of the supernatural. He's just a regular guy, and now he's dealing with all this stuff he knows next to nothing about, all because of that one time he fought evil and won. The way they manage to keep being lighthearted, even in the face of danger, made this book unique …. All in all, a great, enjoyable read."
—Majanka, I Heart Reading Blog

COCAINE ZOMBIES

BRONZE winner in the Mystery/Cozy/Noir category of the 2013 Independent Publishers (IPPY) Book Awards

"A wonderfully written and fun—albeit somewhat scary—new novel…. The three best things about this novel are its fast pace with short chapters, Sam as the likable hero and the humor. 'I wanted to write a book I would also like to read,' Lerner said. 'The characters would talk and act like real people. It would be realistic, but at the same time, larger than life. I didn't want it to follow the same old tired formula.' He succeeded."
—Margo L. Dill, *The News-Gazette*

"A riveting thriller with plenty of twists and turns, very much recommended."
—Midwest Book Review

"Lerner's first-person, hard-boiled narrative—peppered with dark humor and historical and geographical facts pertaining to the Champaign-Urbana setting in which his story unfolds—slyly echoes the work of Jim Thompson, Dashiell Hammett and Raymond Chandler. Fellow Champaign Central High School alum Lerner has crafted a gripping tale, rife with colorful characters, to create a minor masterpiece of modern fiction."
—Don Gerard, Mayor of Champaign, Illinois

"Scott Lerner has created an everyman hero out of small-town lawyer Sam Roberts. Giving Sam a dry wit and gracing him with snappy dialog, Lerner sends him full tilt at the forces of evil that have invaded his humdrum life in Urbana, Illinois. Sam might see himself as a middle-aged schmo, but in Lerner's deft hands, that schmo and his sidekick Bob stumble toward saving the world as we know it. *Cocaine Zombies* is a blast!"
—Molly MacRae, author of *Last Wool and Testament*, *Lawn Order*, and *Wilder Rumors*

"Sam is a character who is easy to root for. He's smart (there are some great-accurate-legal scenes), funny without being sarcastic,

brave without being reckless, and at the end of the day just wants to go back to his one-man law firm and resume his boring life. He's gonna have to go through a lot to get there, however, and it's a very entertaining journey."
—Book Reviews by Elizabeth A. White

"Ladies and Gents, allow me to introduce you to my new best friend: Scott A. Lerner. At a time when I, an avid reader and bookworm extraordinaire, found myself quickly approaching the point of being burnt out after reading book after book until the pages seemed to blend together – I stumbled upon this gem and have found myself putting my game face back on…. Sam is a down to earth lawyer with a sarcastic wit that had me laughing out loud several times while reading. His friend Bob was a man after my own heart – a modern day hippie of sorts. I couldn't help but picture actor Zach Galifianakis as Bob. Both of these men appealed to me because of how down-to-earth they were but also because they were so flippin smart!"
—Not Now … Mommy's Reading

"In *Cocaine Zombies*, Lerner takes the standard legal thriller and throws the rules out the window. With a deft hand and a cutting sense of humor, he crafts a paranormal tale that is both entertaining and disturbing. The triumph of this book is that Lerner takes what could have been a cheap, low grade style thriller and turned it into a subtly nuanced, entertaining read. A job well done."
—Mark Everett Stone, author of the From the Tales of the BSI series and *The Judas Line*

"I couldn't put it down …. It's full of suspense and murder …. This book is by far one of my favorites …. It will send chills up your spine and make you wonder about that little world of voodoo."
—This and That Reviews

THE WICCAN WITCH
OF THE MIDWEST

THE WICCAN WITCH
OF THE MIDWEST

A SAMUEL ROBERTS THRILLER

SCOTT A. LERNER

CAMEL
PRESS
Seattle, WA

Camel Press
PO Box 70515
Seattle, WA 98127

For more information go to: www.camelpress.com
scottlerner.camelpress.com

Cover design by Sabrina Sun

ISBN: 978-1-60381-291-7 (Trade Paper)
ISBN: 978-1-60381-290-0 (eBook)

Library of Congress Control Number: 2015946297

Printed in the United States of America

KENNEDY

To my wife, son, and daughter who have shared some magical times with me. I would also like to thank Fern, Quinn, and Mr. Bay Leaf. I would further like to recognize the creatures that go bump in the night. They help turn Halloween into more than just an opportunity to overindulge.

I would like to praise and acknowledge Catherine Treadgold for her editing skills and all her other efforts to get this book out. A number of red pens died to make this book possible.

Also by the Author

Cocaine Zombies

Ruler of Demons

The Fraternity of the Soul Eater

CHAPTER ONE

~~~

IN LIFE THERE are few fundamental truths. One such truth is that moving sucks. I liked my house. I could walk to work and to the courthouse. My house was located in a historic neighborhood near downtown Urbana. There were homes built during the turn of the century as well as more modern homes that had sprouted up over the years. It was familiar, and the area had antique brick streets lined with old oak trees and plenty of wildlife. If you consider squirrels, rabbits, and birds wildlife.

Yet, it was time to move. There were simply too many bad memories held captive within those walls. A severed head staring up at me from a bed of banana leaves, a tongue set in a silver case, and the hollowed-out remains of a woman lying in my bed. All reminders of what I desperately wanted to forget.

My new house was more modern. It was a cedar-paneled split level backing up to an apple orchard in southwest Champaign. The subdivision was called Rolling Hills—a name that must have been intentionally ironic. Champaign is almost completely flat, thanks to glaciers working their magic millions of years ago. Thus, there are few hills and what hills remain are not exactly rolling. The subdivision next to me is called Cherry Acres but has no cherry trees. There's got to be some guy or gal with a wicked sense of humor in charge of naming subdivisions in Champaign.

I was not just moving away from bad memories. I was running from good ones as well. My girlfriend and the love of my life, Susan, and I spent some wonderful times together in that house. But she'd left me. I wanted no reminders of her and the old house was full of them. I could feel her presence there, as if she were a ghost haunting the place. I sometimes thought I could see her from the corner of my eye or smell her perfume. I was determined to move on.

The movers did most of the work. I borrowed my friend Bob's van to haul away the rest of the boxes. The old house was empty now and all my stuff was mostly squared away in the new house. The closing last week had been uneventful. So much of my past had disappeared with a whimper rather than a bang.

It was my first Saturday in my new digs. I chose this particular house because it made me feel like I was out in the country. The apple orchard out back gives the illusion of space. I did not take into account that it was also a pumpkin patch and at this time of year would be filled with seekers of the great orange squash. Apparently, Halloween draws children and vehicles from all over Champaign County to my backyard, which doesn't actually belong to me, other than the ten feet up to the small fence. The majority of the space belongs to the family who owns the orchard.

A few of the revelers made noises loud enough to be heard in my kitchen. I knew I seemed a bit "bah humbug" and would probably be visited by three ghosts for my lack of Halloween spirit, but lately I had been out of sorts.

Close to a year had passed since my last supernatural entanglement. It had been just as long since Susan broke up with me and an equally long time since I'd had a date. My law practice, which involved everything from handling divorces to representing people in criminal cases, had been dull and my life as a whole uneventful.

I sank into the overstuffed sofa in my sunken living room and turned on the television, which was mounted above a gas fireplace. I felt ridiculous whining about my life. I tried to remember the words of my father, "Suck it up, you Nancy. If you're bored, go out and play." *Damn*, I was surprised I wasn't in need of therapy. Actually I probably did need therapy, but where the hell could I find a therapist who wouldn't have me committed if I told them what I had seen?

I decided to watch *The Shining* on Netflix. I've seen it a million times but it was almost Halloween and it felt right. I had just gotten to the part where the bartender is making suggestions to the caretaker of the inn on his need to better discipline his family when the doorbell rang.

Bob stood on my porch. His curly brown hair looked uncombed, and his goatee was equally untamed. He was wearing a Grateful Dead T-shirt with a skeleton design that looked like early Stanley Mouse. He also wore jeans and Chuck Taylors.

Bob is in his thirties and has put on a little weight over the past couple years, but overall he looks good for his age. I, on the other hand, am starting to look older, my short brown hair gray around the temples. I'm of average height and in pretty good physical condition for being in my late thirties.

"Dude, I was in the neighborhood," Bob said.

"Come on in," I said. "Beer or apple cider?" I stood aside for Bob to enter.

"Alcoholic cider?"

"No."

"Beer."

"Cool."

"Pumpkin ale or Leinenkugel?"

"Surprise me," Bob said.

I went into the kitchen and returned with two pumpkin ales. I handed one to Bob, who was already sitting down and getting into the film. Bob likes almost any movie but he *loves* horror movies.

"So what's up?" I asked.

"The sky, dude. How are you doing?"

"Good, can't complain."

"Can I ask you a personal question?" he said, taking a swig of ale.

"Go ahead, but I may not answer it."

"When was the last time you had a date?"

I sat next to him on the couch. "I assume you are referring to the dried fruit. If not, that question is a bit personal."

"Don't answer. I know the answer. You haven't had a date since Susan left. Dude, life is short. Get out there, enjoy yourself."

I wrinkled my nose in disbelief. "I don't need a girlfriend to enjoy life. I have a television and a kitchen full of snacks. As the great Bob Marley once said, 'no woman no sad' or something like that."

"Didn't Ziggy Marley say, 'Love can't bring bad things, only good things'?" Bob said. "Wait, I don't think that's quite right."

I shook my head. "I have no idea. Who would quote Ziggy Marley?"

Bob threw up his hands, almost spilling his ale. "Dude, you need a change of scenery to get out and embrace life. You need to come with me to the Grand Pumpkin Plot in beautiful Arthur, Illinois."

"My backyard backs up into a pumpkin patch."

"This one has more varieties of pumpkins as well as pumpkin pie, pumpkin ice cream, and pumpkin muffins. Besides, what else were you planning to do today?"

"Do I need to change?"

"Yes, but the clothing you're wearing is fine. It's casual."

"All right," I said, clicking off the movie. "I do love pumpkin-based foods."

I was wearing gray sweatpants and a white T-shirt. I grabbed a leather jacket and we were ready to go. We took my Honda and headed south on the highway toward Tuscola.

It was a beautiful fall day. The fields were mostly harvested with a few straggler farmers out on a perfect Saturday afternoon gathering the remaining corn and soybeans. Dust hung heavy in the air and a few remaining harvesters were at work in the fields.

We pulled off I-57 and took the Arcola exit to Arthur, where we passed a number of black single-horse buggies with orange triangles on the back. About an hour after we had left, we pulled into the Grand Pumpkin Plot.

Bob had not exaggerated with regard to this place. There were wooden crates filled with all manner of pumpkins, squash, and gourds. Also hayrides and an extensive corn maze. Bob insisted on hitting the restaurant first.

For being in the middle of nowhere, the restaurant was surprisingly large. Bob had the pumpkin soup with pumpkin quiche while I opted for the pumpkin ravioli. We split the pumpkin cheesecake for dessert. Afterward I felt kind of sick of pumpkin, but Bob ordered a pumpkin latte.

I wanted to get my pumpkin from the field while Bob was satisfied with digging through the crates. So I headed into the field past the corn maze. It was surprisingly large—had to be over twenty acres—but also surprisingly empty. Other than the group of people on the hay-filled trailer being dragged behind a large tractor, it was empty.

I was kneeling over a potential jack-o-lantern when I heard the loud squawking of crows in the air. A moment later twenty crows alighted on separate pumpkins all around me. Each bird was staring at me. I don't like black birds. I don't trust crows, ravens, or grackles. It's not that I'm a bird racist; only, black birds always seem to precede the coming of dark supernatural forces in my life. In the past it had always been a single bird, maybe two. If the number of birds had a bearing on the proportional strength of the evil force to come, then I was screwed.

I returned to the area where I'd left Bob, trying to figure

out if what I'd seen was some sort of sign. I found Bob closely examining a large Cinderella pumpkin.

"Dude, did you forget something?" Bob asked.

"What?"

"A pumpkin."

"No, nothing worked for me."

"Damn, if you are as picky about potential dates as you are about pumpkins, then you will never find true love."

"Can we change the subject?"

"Sure." He paused. "So, do you ever worry about what will happen in the future?"

"Why bother worrying about what no one knows? Although, that is kind of an odd subject to bring up out of nowhere."

"I know someone who foretells the future. A woman so beautiful that flowers call her up for beauty tips. A woman so wise that owls call her up for advice. A woman who will reveal your future."

I blew out an exasperated puff of air. "You sound like a bad infomercial. Are you serious?"

"As a heart attack. I'm told she is uncanny. I have an appointment. Come on, keep me company. It will take ten minutes to get there."

"You had this planned the whole time, didn't you?"

"Of course."

"That's a hell of a pitch," I said. "She must be great looking. How do you know she is so good if you've only been told she is 'uncanny'?"

"You know that girl I was seeing last year?"

"The one with big hair who wore way too much makeup?"

"Crystal, and yes, that's the one. I went there with her once. Everything she was told in her reading came to pass."

"You mean the great fortune teller predicted she would dump you and start dating that Neanderthal?"

Bob folded his arms defensively. "Brad, and yes, among other things."

"You do realize that she might have broken up with you because the fortune teller told her she would and she trusted the fortune teller, right? Maybe it was a self-fulfilling prophecy."

"She also predicted Crystal would lose her job and have an allergic reaction to shellfish. Both came to pass."

"It did not take a fortune teller to predict that Crystal would lose her job. Hell, it was a miracle she had a job. The shellfish thing, however, was pretty good."

"She is psychic," he insisted.

"Fine," I said, "I will go to watch her reveal your destiny."

We paid our bill and filled the back of the car with Bob's pumpkin-related purchases. In less than five minutes we were back on the road. Before we drove off, I noticed that it was beginning to get colder and the sky looked like rain.

"Where are we headed?"

"Believe it or not, there is a village populated by witches in the heart of Amish Country."

"You know I don't believe in fortune tellers and witches."

"You also don't believe in voodoo spirits, the devil, demons, and Egyptian Gods, but they all believe in you," Bob said. "Besides, there are a million fortune tellers and witches online. They do exist."

"I believe in fortune tellers," I said. "I just don't believe they can foretell the future. I believe in witches and Wicca as it relates to being a religion. I just don't believe in magic."

He snorted. "You are so full of it," he said. "We have seen too much magic for you not to believe in it."

"Fine." I pulled over so some maniac could pass. "I believe in magic, witches, and fortune tellers. I just don't believe you found a group of people in Central Illinois with these powers."

"You will believe before the day is done, Grasshopper," Bob said in a decent imitation of Kwai Chang Caine from *Kung Fu*.

We turned down a number of roads until we saw a village in the distance surrounded by harvested fields. Finally we arrived at a large, purple, three-story Victorian home.

Bob pulled into the driveway. There were at least five other Victorian homes in the village that I could see and ten or so other houses in different designs and from different eras, all backed up to an oblong communal area. The communal area had two unpainted wood gazebos and a fire pit, but was mostly open. We got out of the car and walked up to the house. Three stairs led up to a white porch. At the large oak door, Bob struck a brass knocker in the shape of a lion. In less than a minute the door opened.

CHAPTER TWO

~~~

THE WOMAN WHO came to the door was tall, with long black hair that fell to her waist and intense blue eyes that resembled a Siamese cat's. With her pale skin and high cheekbones, she might have been part Scottish and part Native American. She wore a simple black dress, and her only jewelry was a silver pentacle on a silver chain. Bob had not overstated her beauty.

"Bob, it's good to see you," the woman said, giving him a hug.

"You must be Sam, the man whose future is in question," she said without touching me.

"Well, actually …."

I was about to set her straight, but she'd already opened the door and waved us in, so I let it go for now. The interior was inviting, with an eclectic mix of furniture and knickknacks that somehow all went together. I admired the tiger oak floor and the imposing wooden staircase directly before us. On our left was a room filled with potted plants. A maroon velvet sofa and two matching chairs faced an enormous picture window divided into three sections that must have been added to the home a hundred years after it was built. To the right was an old fashioned parlor, which contained a sofa and six wooden chairs, none of them matching, and a number of tables. Next to the sofa was a table of ornately carved mahogany with a marble top. An old maple tea table stood between two chairs and an oak parlor table between two other chairs. All the furniture was wooden and antique in a hodgepodge of styles, and the colors were warm shades of red and pink. The lamps had fringed shades and the pottery looked handmade. There were a few porcelain figurines of animals, mostly wolves and cats in different positions of rest, along with various pieces of folk art representing the moon and sun. I wondered if these were part of her seasonal décor or a sly reference to her profession.

"Can I get you some tea? To drink, that is. I don't use tea leaves for divination. A skill I have yet to acquire." She turned to Bob. "I don't need to be a fortune teller to know you did not tell your friend why he is here."

"I told him you were a fortune teller. I wanted my gift of a reading to be a surprise. I lied and told him it was for me," Bob said.

"The spirits tell me your veracity should be questioned. You did not intend to surprise him with a gift. You just didn't want him to say no." To me, she said, "My name's Bridget Gillis. Bob felt you were uneasy about what the future has in store for you. Most people are. I also sense that you are not a believer. Although, when Bob called to speak with me, he made it clear that you have stepped into the word of the supernatural enough times that you can't completely dismiss my calling. Besides, Bob must have told you how accurate my reading for his ... friend Crystal was."

Bob sat forward in his chair, eager as a puppy dog. "She really can tell the future. Give it a try," he said.

"You said you were getting a reading, not me. Maybe she's right and it is not a matter of my questioning her skills. Maybe I just don't want to know."

"You're not a little curious?" Bob said. "What is the worst

that can happen? We get a good laugh and go on our way. I'm paying," he added.

"I think the worst that could happen is that I will be told I am going to die in the morning," I said, taking his words literally.

"That's not so awful. You'd still die, whether you knew about it or not. At least by knowing we could have some fun before you went. I could throw a party."

I threw up my hands. "Fine, I'll go along with it, but it's all crazy."

Bridget laid a soft hand on my arm. "Don't feel obligated on my account, Sam. I would love to do your reading, but I won't be offended if you refuse. There are many people who are uncomfortable knowing about their destinies."

When she removed her hand, I felt its absence somehow. She had a certain something about her. Maybe it was just her beauty, or maybe I was sensing her power. For men it is often difficult to separate beauty from anything else.

"Do your readings always come to pass?" I asked.

"Given the nature of free will, the future can be changed. That said, in practical terms, it rarely is. I record my readings in my Book of Shadows. I never put down names, to protect my clients' privacy. Yet, when clients come back to discuss the aftermath of my readings, I am rarely, if ever, wrong." She looked at Bob. "Have you found that to be true?" she asked.

"Crystal said you were right on," Bob said. "Although, I wish you hadn't been. I do miss her."

"It is for the best. Trust me on that," Bridget said.

"Fine," I said, shifting uncomfortably in my seat, "you've talked me into it. What are we going to do? Crystal ball, palm reading?"

"How about a simple Tarot card reading? Bob said you are looking for love. Let's find out what we can see. Maybe get a clue as to the direction your life is taking you in."

"I can predict that if Bob keeps discussing my love life with strangers, his future will be short," I said.

"Bob, why don't you show Mr. Roberts to the reading room while I prepare the tea? As you are aware, guests are not invited to observe a reading. Once we get started, you can retire to the solarium."

Bob led me to a wooden door against the far back wall of the room with the plants and windows. I assume this was the 'solarium,' even though I had never referred to a room as such in my life. This door led to a narrow hallway with a number of doors. Bob led me to the first door on the right and we walked in.

The room was fairly small. Built into the wall on the left was an enormous glass front china cabinet. The glass was stained dark purple and green, which concealed its contents. Against the wall to my right was a mahogany hutch with an oil painting of an old woman above it. In the middle of the room was a small table covered with a black velvet tablecloth. A bag of black cloth sat on top of the table, a wooden chair on each side. I suspected that this was where the reading would take place. Next to the larger table was a smaller piecrust tea table with a flame mahogany top.

The room had no windows or natural lighting, and the chandelier cast a dim light. It was so old, I wondered if it had been converted from gas. The arms of the chandelier looked like branches of a tree, with small bulbs at the ends.

"I can't believe you talked me into this," I said to Bob.

"To paraphrase Bob Dylan, having nothing means nothing to lose."

"Yes, but I do have my dignity."

"Dignity?"

I grimaced. "Oh shut up. I know the only reason I'm here is because the fortune teller is hot as hell. You found the only fortune teller in Illinois who is not an old gypsy lady with a scarf over her head and one hoop earring."

Just as the words left my mouth, the fortune teller reentered the room caring a silver tray with a Wedgewood porcelain tea set. She set it down on the tea table.

"Please go on, Mr. Roberts. You were just saying how 'hot' I am compared to others in my profession," Bridget Gillis said without cracking a smile.

"I'm sorry. I didn't realize you could hear me."

"Of course, but obviously you are not sorry for what you said, only for what I heard. Please have a seat, Mr. Roberts." She waved her arm toward the chair in front of the table. I sat down with my face bent so she wouldn't see me blush.

She poured Bob a cup of tea and placed two biscuits on the saucer; then Bob left the room without having to be dismissed. She poured me a cup as well, and I took a couple of biscuits. The tea smelled of cut grass and fallen leaves. It tasted sweet, like honeysuckles and warm summer days.

CHAPTER THREE

~~~

"**W**HAT WONDERFUL TEA. Thank you."

"Now you're just being nice because of your earlier comments," she said, settling into the chair across from me.

She removed a wooden box from the black bag on the table. The box was polished rosewood with no designs cut into it to disturb the grain of the wood. Inside was an old deck of cards. She carefully removed the cards and placed them in front of her.

"So what do you know of the Tarot?" she asked.

"Tarot cards can be used to tell the future," I said. "Solitaire used them in *Live and Let Die* until she and 007 made love. Then she lost her powers."

"Okay, so I can assume you know nothing about Tarot. Tarot cards have been used since the fifteenth century as playing cards. In the 1700s people started using them for divination. The deck in front of you came from Europe. It has been in my family for over a hundred years."

"I will try not to bend any of the corners," I said.

"Thanks. Twenty-two of the cards are known as the Major Arcana. They are the Magician, the High Priestess, the Empress, the Emperor, the Hierophant, the Lovers, the Chariot, Strength, the Hermit, Wheel of Fortune, Justice, the Hanged Man,

Death, Temperance, the Devil, the Tower, the Star, the Moon, the Sun, Judgment, the World, and the Fool." She named these very quickly, as if by rote, while sorting through the deck. She found the particular cards she was looking for and set them in front of me. "Here are the cards for the Devil and Death."

I pointed at the card for the devil—a winged creature with the lower body of a goat and the upper body of a man. He sat on a perch of some kind with a naked man and woman chained before him. The Death card was even scarier, with a skeleton in armor on a white horse holding on to a black and white flag. It looked like Albrecht Dürer's famous etching of a knight traveling through the valley of death.

"Shit. I hope those guys don't show up in my reading," I said.

"That is why I'm pointing them out. The symbols do not necessary represent their true meaning. 'Death' can be a good card. It may mean that you will be freed from the darkness around you and will have a new, more positive future. 'The Devil' may similarly provide a positive message."

"That is good to know."

"I should also note that the direction of the card has meaning. A card facing you tends to have a completely different meaning if it is upside down. Usually it is better if the card is right side up. Usually but not always.

"There are also the Minor Arcana. In my deck there are fifty-six of these cards, divided into four suits of fourteen cards each—ten numbered cards and four court cards. The court cards are the King, Queen, Knight, and Jack, in each of the four Tarot suits. In my deck the suits are swords, wands, pentacles, and cups." As she spoke she moved the cards around with the facility of a Vegas dealer.

"I intend to start with the simplest reading," she continued. "If you have questions about your love life or any other matters we can address that next. Before I start, I want you to hold the cards. You need not shuffle them, although some readers suggest that. I do not. I simply want you to hold them and think about what you want them to tell us."

The cards felt cold and ancient. I knew it was probably because of their odd images combined with this strange environment, but they felt otherworldly somehow, and they smelled a bit like sage. After a long moment, the fortune teller took them out of my hands and began to shuffle them.

"I intend to give you the simplest of readings. I will lay out four cards and flip them over one at a time, explaining their meaning. The first card will represent the past, meaning your past. The second card represents your current situation. The third card represents the future. The fourth represents what will be the result should your path remain unchanged. We have free will, so the future is not set in stone, but it rarely changes.

"The Major Arcana have more of an influence than the Minor Arcana. Obviously if there are fifty-six cards of the Minor Arcana and twenty-two cards of the Major Arcana, you are far more likely to see cards from the Minor Arcana."

She finished shuffling. She had long, tapered fingers, and they moved like a cellar spider's legs as she removed the top four cards from the deck and spread them out in front of me. Although I was not a believer, I felt a growing sense of anticipation. I expected more of a mysterious vibe, but she seemed so matter-of-fact. She was confident and did not feel the need to impress or convince me of anything.

She lifted the first card and flipped it over. It depicted a medieval tower being struck by lightning. Flames licked the top of the tower and two people were falling to their death. It was in the reverse position.

"The Tower represents destruction and darkness," she explained. "In some cases it may also lead to a new beginning, but it does not always. This is your past—what you have already dealt with. I suspect you have seen great evil and survived it. In the past you have been involved with some dark forces and you are struggling to decide whether to continue in your present path or find some other direction. Perhaps the other cards will shed light on your circumstances."

I pointed at the card and grimaced. "That is my past?"

"Yes. If it were your future, I'd be concerned. Yet, you have already fought through it and survived."

She flipped the second card.

It was the ten of swords. A man lay face down in the dirt, pinned to the ground by ten swords. I could tell by the look on the face of the fortune teller this was not good.

"The ten of swords can represent destruction but …" her voice trailed off.

This could not be good. "Are you okay?"

"Yes, this card represents your present. In some ways you are already trapped. I suspect evil is trying to hold you in place. I can't guess beyond that."

She flipped the third card to reveal the Devil in the reverse position.

"I'm glad you told me earlier that The Devil is not necessarily bad," I joked.

"The Devil often indicates an addiction or obsession. The fact that it is in the reverse position is not the opposite of the regular position. As I told you earlier, the position of the card can change its meaning. It is too early to be concerned and I can't be sure what it foretells until the last card puts it into context."

"Is an addiction or obsession always bad?"

"Not always, but in your case it appears to be a struggle with darkness. Yet, let's wait for the last card before we try and interpret its meaning."

As she spoke she flipped over the final card. I was not surprised to see Death. It was in the upright position.

"Wow, you are psychic," I said, trying to lighten the mood. "You pull out two cards ahead of time and they both come up."

"The final position represents how you will deal with the future. Death can open the door to new beginnings. It is not a bad card. My guess is you are learning to deal with the darkness that has been haunting your past. And yes, it is not a bad card."

As she spoke her voice cracked. She was visibly shaken. Her reaction seemed inconsistent with her words. Was she so afraid for my future? She didn't even know me.

"You know," she said, giving her head a little shake, "I don't think the cards were shuffled well after my last use. Can we try again after I give them a good shuffle?" She picked up all the cards, including the four left on the table. She shuffled them for a few minutes and then quickly placed four new cards in front of me. She dropped a few cards as she shuffled, quickly adding them back into her deck. Her hands were shaking. She should be glad her game was Tarot and not Poker. She was clearly unable to hide her emotions.

She flipped the first card. It was the Tower. She flipped the second to reveal the Ten of Swords in the upright position. She flipped the remaining two cards: the Devil and Death. The cards were just as they had been. This was either a really good trick or a strange coincidence.

She looked at me and reached over and touched my hands that had been resting on the table. When we touched it felt like an electric charge was running through me. It may have been static electricity but it felt like more than that. Then I looked at the fortune teller. Her eyes had rolled back into her head so that I could see nothing of her bright blue irises. She seemed to be in another place and time. Then, in an instant, she was back.

"L-look," she stammered, her pale skin taking on a green tinge, "there will be no charge for my services. I am not feeling well." She stood up. She seemed slightly off balance as she walked with me back to the front room. Bob got up from his chair.

"Are you two all right?" he asked.

"Fine," she said, "I just have a migraine. There will be no charge. Thank you for coming such a long way." She turned and walked unsteadily through a door in the back of the room. Bob and I let ourselves out.

As we opened the front door a black cat forced its way inside.

The cat looked up at me and hissed. Once inside she raised her back and hissed again, baring her sharp teeth. I was glad to exit this strange house. I wondered if the cat was a sign of bad luck or a familiar returning to its mistress.

CHAPTER FOUR

~~~

"That was weird," I said.

"Yeah," Bob said, "I could tell. What happened?"

I told him what I had observed but didn't share what I had felt—that something had passed between myself and the fortune teller when we touched. She seemed to have had a premonition, and not a good one.

"Did she react that way when Crystal had her reading done?" I asked.

"No. If she had, I wouldn't have brought you here."

"That's was really odd," I said.

"No shit," Bob agreed.

"I hope she isn't truly psychic, because if she saw my future, it doesn't look too bright."

Bob shuddered. "Mine either. Whenever you get into trouble it doesn't bode well for me. I still remember my near death in a hot tub."

I smiled. "At least you almost died with one of the most attractive woman I have ever seen."

"Not any hotter than the fortune teller. Bridget can read my cards in bed anytime."

"Man, that is sexist, even for you. That said, if you go for that tall mysterious type she is rather—"

"Smoking?" Bob broke in. "So hot you would drink her father's bathwater?"

I gave him a reproving look. "I was going to say she is rather attractive, if that's your type."

"What type would that be … human? You haven't had a single date since you and Susan broke up. You need to get out there."

"Hey, I have an idea," I said, "why don't we check out this cool village and move on from talking about my love life or lack thereof? Besides, I prefer less drama. Bridget may be attractive but she is clearly disturbed. I would prefer someone less attractive and more … normal."

"Fine. I think there are three or four shops around here. I've wanted to check them out but never took the time."

We walked around the back of the fortune teller's home, where there was a long oblong field we'd noticed earlier. The outer edge of the field was surrounded by homes from different eras. To the right were three buildings that looked like the storefronts in an old Western. They were similar to shotgun houses, but it was clear from the signage that they were simple structures used for shops. A wooden sidewalk connected the three stores. At the far end of the field was a flat-roofed structure that must have been a community meeting hall when the village was first built.

We headed toward the shops. The first sold candles and herbs. A wooden sign had the words CRAFT STORE carved over a crescent moon.

"I assume this is the front of the store because of the sign, but the other side would have access to the road. That is a little weird, don't you think?"

"I can think of a lot stranger stuff about the store than that," Bob said as we stepped onto the wooden sidewalk and opened the glass and wood door. A bell announced our presence.

The store smelled of herbs and fresh earth. A girl-next-door cheerleader type with long blonde hair, a heart-shaped face, and blue eyes greeted us. She was pleasant and upbeat. Her clothing was the opposite of cheerleader—modest and feminine with a lot of gauzy fabric, like a costume from an early twentieth century modern dance performance.

"Hello, and welcome, my name is Wendy. Thank you for coming. Is there something in particular you're looking for?"

"We're just browsing," I said. "I had my fortune told next door so we were in the neighborhood."

"Bridget is very good," Wendy said.

"Do you get a lot of customers this far out?" I asked.

"No, mostly online. Are you Wiccan, Witches, or just having fun?"

"Is there a difference?"

"Yes," she said with a straight face, "you can have fun playing catch."

"No, between Wiccans and Witches."

She folded her hands in front of her as if about to speak before a large audience. "Yes, Wicca is a diverse religion that brings together elements of pagan beliefs and elements of witchcraft. It has only been around since the 1950s. Witches have been around since the time of the caveman. This community was founded well over a hundred years ago."

"So you are a witch?" Bob asked.

"Of course," the woman said.

"A community of witches in the middle of Amish Country. Doesn't that offend the Amish?" I asked.

"It might have, a hundred years ago. Now we all kind of mind our own business. Yet you don't have to be a witch to enjoy herbs and candles. I also sell corn brooms." Wendy picked one up to show us.

"Can you fly on them?" Bob asked.

I elbowed Bob but his comment didn't seem to faze the woman.

"No, just for cleaning the kitchen floor. They are mostly Amish-made. A couple of the brooms come from Arcola, the home of the Arcola Broom Corn Festival. I'm afraid we don't fly brooms or wear pointy black hats." She cocked her head and added, "Although, on occasion, if someone disrespects our beliefs, turning them into a toad is not out of the question."

I laughed, but Bob did not. This woman clearly could hold her own.

I looked over the long counter at the rows and rows of dried herbs in glass jars. She had an old brass NCR candy store cash register that looked to be from the turn of the century. There were ropes tied across the opposite wall strung with bouquets of herbs and tapered candles on strings. In the middle of the room was a free standing shelf full of unusual items. There were pillar candles of all types, along with crystals and spell books bound in leather. I found a thick pillar candle of pure beeswax and decided to purchase it—in part because I love the smell of burning beeswax candles and in part to make up for Bob's rude comment.

"What about the other stores?" I asked as she wrapped the candle in newspaper.

"My next door neighbor is Alice, who sells unusual food items. She has a lot of organic meat, fruit, and vegetables, which she also sells online. The last store is owned by Mr. Levi. He sells antique books and manuscripts. Both stores are worth seeing."

"Thanks for the candle."

"I put my card in the bag with my website listed if you decide to order something else. I also put in a flyer about how to use the candle. You might want to light it for Samhain or Halloween, depending on what you call it. We ordinarily have a bonfire and invite the public to our village, but not this year. It's a special year for us so outsiders are not welcome. You should have been here for Mabon. It was a good year for the harvest, and a great celebration."

We left the store and walked next door to an identical building with hams hanging in the plate glass window. This was the store owned by Alice as was made clear by the sign that read ALICE'S FINE FOODS. Alice was in her thirties, with straight brown hair tied in a single braid that hung down her back. She was objectively pretty, but there was something mean looking about her. Perhaps it was the lines around her mouth. She looked like she was used to frowning, despite the smile she greeted us with. She wore a simple black dress with a white apron favored by butchers. I was instantly reminded of my third grade teacher. That is not a compliment; my third grade teacher was as mean as a snake. I still remember the time she denied me a fig newton during snack time because I wouldn't sit still during her reading of *James and the Giant Peach*.

Although the store was identical in dimensions and architectural design to the one owned by Wendy, the interior was completely different. A large chrome refrigerator case stood in place of Wendy's countertop. Above the case were pigs' legs hanging from hooks. The legs looked like the type found in Spain with their hooves still attached. The glass case was filled with cheeses and smoked meat and fish. Shelves throughout the store were filled with snacks from all over the world. She also sold imported chocolates, spices, and oils.

"How can I help you?" Alice asked.

"We are just looking around," I said.

Bob had already located a handmade wooden basket and was filling it with various items.

"All chocolate is twenty percent off. What brings you here, the fortune teller or the pumpkins?"

"Both."

"Well, I like seeing customers in person. It seems like most of my business is online nowadays."

She acted more pleasant than she looked. I had to assume based on the chocolate selection that she wasn't all bad. Then again she was probably being pleasant on account of Bob. Bob was proving to be an excellent customer.

Twenty minutes later Bob had spent a hundred and twenty-five dollars and filled about a third of a single brown paper bag. He seemed pleased with his purchases. We walked out of the store and down the wooden sidewalk to the last store, the book store of Mr. Levi.

The store had a carved wooden sign depicting an owl with RAYMOND LEVI, FINE BOOKS written below. It contained a number of glass cases displaying old parchments and scrolls. The walls of the entire store were lined in book cases filled with newer books as well as worn, leather-bound volumes. In the middle of the room was an Amish-made wooden table surrounded by a number of chairs. I picked up a leather book on the table and opened the cover. There was a bookplate with an etching of an owl and the words '*Ex Libre* Raymond Levi' on the inside cover. It was titled *Spells of Nature*.

"Welcome to my store, gentleman. I am afraid the book you just picked up is part of my personal collection, but I do have similar volumes for sale." Mr. Levi spoke with a very proper English accent and would have made an excellent mad professor in a fifties horror movie. He was tall with a graying beard, and his salt and pepper hair was short and curly. He wore gold wire-rimmed glasses.

"Thank you," I said.

Mr. Levi walked with a peculiarly clipped gait over to one of the shelves and picked up a book. "We have some grimoires that go back to the sixteenth century. I have a page from a Book of Shadows that allegedly belonged to Agnes Sampson."

"Who is that?" Bob asked.

"She was a Scottish Midwife in the late sixteenth century. She was later burnt at the stake. I have had the document dated, and it was clearly created at the right time and place, but the provenance linking it to her is a bit sketchy. The person I bought it from claims to be a relative and further will swear it is the genuine article. That said, it is priced at only five thousand dollars. If authenticated it would be priceless."

"What is a grimoire and a Book of Shadows?"

Mr. Levi waved his hands in the air in a gesture of complaisance. "Oh I *am* sorry; I assumed you were warlocks or collectors. A grimoire contains spells or instructions related to magic rituals. Some give directions for making talismans—magic objects. I have a few that go back hundreds of years. Although most of my collection is from the nineteenth century. A Book of Shadows is similar, as it contains religious texts and rituals. However, the concept did not come about until the twentieth century, as it relates to Wiccan beliefs."

"Like in *Charmed*?" Bob asked.

"No. My belief system has nothing to do with a television show featuring scantily clad women pretending to understand the sacred," Mr. Levi responded rather stiffly.

"Sorry," I interjected, "no offense was intended."

"Perhaps, if you don't intend to make a purchase, you could find somewhere else to spend your time."

"Fuck off," Bob said, leaving the store.

I followed after. Bob seemed more upset than I thought was reasonable.

"Don't you thing that was a bit over the top?" I asked, once we reached the car.

"He was rude, pompous, and disrespected a good television show," Bob said.

"Yet, you allowed him to live."

"I guess I am just tired."

CHAPTER FIVE

~~~

W E GOT INTO the car and began to make our way back to I-57. On this route the fields had a somewhat different look, most of the crops in grain bins or in trucks. Some had partial stalks still standing with dried leaves on the ground. A few farmers had managed to remove even the partial stalks, leaving an ocean of dark soil. Illinois farmers are the beneficiaries of borrowed top soil from melting glaciers over a hundred thousand years ago. As a result, Central Illinois has some of the most fertile soil in the world. Many of the fields were filled with Canadian Geese lucky enough to get a free meal of the corn that the farmers missed. They would have to compete with deer and crows.

We had traveled about a half a mile when we passed an old white farm house. A wooden sign in the front yard advertised fresh eggs, jam, and jellies. A black Amish buggy was parked in the driveway, no horse in sight.

"Dude, let's get some jam and apple butter," Bob said.

"Cool, maybe some pumpkin butter would be nice as well."

We parked in the driveway and walked up to a large red barn, where we found a chalkboard sign with a handwritten list of jams. A bearded man with no mustache in his late thirties or early forties came out to greet us with a laconic, "Good day." He wore a plain blue shirt, black pants, and a straw hat. Following close behind him was a small girl in a blue dress and white bonnet and carrying a faceless rag doll. She must have been three or four.

The man led us into a barn and indicated a long shelf with rows of jars containing jellies, jams, and fruit butter. An old 1950s refrigerator bore a label that said CHEESES AND MILK.

"I didn't think the Amish had electricity or refrigeration," Bob said to me.

"I don't know what the rule is," I replied.

"It varies from community to community," the man said. "The elders have allowed us to have refrigeration in this outbuilding for the purpose of storing milk and cheese. Our community produces a lot of cheese."

"I went to the cheese festival last Labor Day weekend in Arthur," Bob said.

I picked out a small wheel of baby Swiss cheese. Bob chose two jars of apple butter.

"You know, I'm surprised that the woman at the village didn't sell this stuff," Bob said to me.

"You went to the village up the road. The village of the damned," the man said, his voice cracking. The little girl grabbed the man's leg, as if afraid of us.

"No," Bob said, "it's a small village maybe a mile or two up the road. There is a fortune teller and a couple of weird shops."

"You two are not welcome here," the man said, more fearful than angry. "Put back the items you have selected and please leave."

We put back our items and returned to the car. By the time we got there, the bearded man had emerged from the barn carrying a shotgun. We pulled out of the driveway.

"I thought the Amish believed in non-violence," Bob said. "The live-and-let-live type."

I looked back where the man had stood, but he'd gone back inside. "Me too. I'm thinking that guy does not like that village."

"That seems like an understatement," Bob said. "He called it 'the village of the damned.' "

"Wasn't that a movie?"

Bob is a living, breathing movie database, at least for horror films. You could always count on him to supply the details without having to look them up.

"Actually two," he said. "There was an English movie from the 1960s with that title and then a remake in the 1980s, directed by John Carpenter."

"Wow, if you used the brain space you have dedicated to old movies to finding a cure for cancer, the world would be a better place."

"I doubt the brain space could rise to that level," Bob said.

"Good point," I replied.

"I did see a movie about a guy who found the cure for cancer."

"Any good?"

"It was all right."

We drove home in relative silence. I was thinking about the fortune teller. In part I was wondering what it would be like to make love to such a beautiful and mysterious woman. I could imagine having sex with her easier than I could imagine hanging out with her. She seemed so intense. My imagination would not allow me to envision sitting around and watching a movie with her. Besides, I'd all but given up on dating. My life was too chaotic. I couldn't go through what happened between Susan and me again. It was as if my heart had been pulled from my chest, leaving nothing but hollowness. I felt like the woman I'd found in my bed last year with her insides removed in a bastardization of an Ancient Egyptian mummification ceremony.

Because of her association with me, Susan had almost died more than once. Everyone who hung out with me was at risk. Bob too.

Most of all I was thinking about what happened when the fortune teller and I touched. Did she have a premonition about my future? Had the cards told her something she didn't share? Did I even believe in fortune tellers?

I drove us both back to my new home, and Bob took off for his place. The new digs were comfortable and beginning to feel familiar. No one had died here, to my knowledge, and that was certainly a bonus.

It was strange confronting the supernatural again … if having your fortune read is supernatural. I guess it depends on whether you believe the fortune teller has genuine power. Bob said she'd read his old girlfriend's fortune, but he wasn't there for the actual reading. At least I assumed he wasn't, since Bob had not been allowed in the room for my reading. I suspect Bob was more interested in the fortune teller than the actual fortune told. Thus, his opinion of her skills was suspect.

It was after six in the evening and cool outside. My new living room had a gas fireplace that lit up with the touch of a remote control. That was kind of nice.

I went into the kitchen to look for something to eat and decided on a frozen spinach soufflé. It would take more than an hour to cook but I had time. I decided to lie down for a bit on the puffy leather sofa. I tried to clear my mind of the strangeness of the day. It didn't take long for sleep to come.

CHAPTER SIX

~~~

I AWOKE TO find myself in a cornfield surrounded by men and women. The men wore black or brown jackets with breeches and garters along with felt, flat-topped hats with large brims. Some of the hats had buckles. Most of the men had ruffs around their necks. The women were clad in simple dresses with bonnets and matching white collars. Some also wore aprons.

I thought about the Amish family I had just seen. Yet these people didn't look Amish, more as though they came from the past. The world did not seem any different than it had the day before. I wondered how I could determine the year with so few clues—only strangely dressed people standing in a field. It's not as if I knew anything about how people dressed in any particular historical period. I looked for signs of technology— telephone lines or lights—in the distance and saw none.

The people had gathered around me and I found myself walking along with them toward something in the middle of the field. A pretty young woman in her late teens brushed against me.

"Pray pardon me. It is my first burning and I do not wish to miss a moment."

I turned to respond but she had already passed me by.

"What cheer, to see such a sight on All Hallow's Eve!" a man said, pushing ahead of me.

In a moment I was standing before a pile of logs and sticks. In the center of the pile was a large stake, and tied to that stake was a naked woman—the fortune teller. Her body was covered in sweat and she seemed to glow in the moonlight. The silver necklace with the pentagram hung around her neck. There was a tattoo just below her left breast of the symbols from the Tarot—a cup, a wand, a sword, and a pentacle.

As I looked on, someone threw a flaming branch onto the sticks and logs. I was so mesmerized by the beauty of the woman's body that it was not until her flesh began to burn that I became aware of the horror of the scene before me. Her skin turned red and then black. Her long dark hair began to burn and I could smell it in the air. Her eyes, once so beautiful and clear, seemed to melt from their sockets.

A man walked up to the flames and turned to face us all. He was older, with a beard, and I recognized him at once. It was Mr. Levi from the bookstore. He spoke in a commanding tone. This was the leader of the group.

"We are here to present a burnt offering for our Lord. It is a gift for the King of Kings. The witch is dead. Let her spirit return to hell where she will reside as Satan's harlot."

After a bit the ghastly smell of burnt hair and accelerant died away, replaced by the smell of the burnt wood and flesh. I was reminded of a barbecue, which was more abhorrent than the earlier, more acrid odors. I awoke as the odor grew stronger.

My soufflé was starting to burn. I got up and ran to the kitchen. My new kitchen had stainless steel appliances. The Wolf Stove was one of the reasons I bought the house. That and the granite Uba Tuba countertops … along with the fact that the refrigerator has never contained human body parts.

The dream had definitely shaken me up. I was starting to notice a pattern in my encounters with the supernatural. The black birds and then the dream all fit into that pattern. I would not have been surprised if the Angel of Death or a vampire had come a-calling at that moment.

If a vampire did stop by, it wouldn't be good. I wasn't a tween and I doubted it would be one of those wimpy vampires that sparkle in the daylight. With my luck I would get one of those rip-your-throat-out types.

My guess is that vampires can't be real because they would already have taken over the world. They would be too smart, too fast, and too strong for us to eradicate. Humans would be chained in the refrigerated section of the grocery store, long straws attached to our sides like large, blood-filled juice boxes.

I was thinking about calling Bob to tell him my dream when the telephone rang. It was Bob.

"Dude, you want to come over and watch a flick tonight?"

"It's Saturday night," I said. "I would have figured you already had a date. Especially since you made fun of me for not getting out much since Susan and I called it quits."

"Number one, I believe it was Susan who called it quits. Number two, I would rather spend quality time with you. That, and I just got a call from Heather, the girl I had a date with tonight. She had some kind of hair emergency and couldn't make it."

"And you believed her?"

"Dude, that's harsh."

"Gee," I said, "you do know how to make a guy feel special. Second choice to Heather. So what is the movie *de jour*?"

"Given our day, I thought we could watch, *Children of the Corn* and *The Craft*."

"What, no *Village of the Damned* or *The Crucible*?"

"You know, I have never seen *The Crucible*," Bob said, as if confessing to a misdeed.

"No, me neither. I know it was based on a play and had something to do with the Salem Witch Trials. I think it was meant as an allegory relating to McCarthy and the whole communist scare of the 1950s. Does that make it an allegory or a metaphor? I never know what term to use."

"I hate metaphors. A metaphor in a film is a tick sucking the fun out."

"Yeah, I hate them as well. Metaphors are the gum at the bottom of the table at a restaurant. They are just icky."

" 'Icky'? Damn, you need to get a date. You are losing touch with reality."

"What time is the damn movie?"

"How about in an hour?"

"I'll see you then."

I sat down and ate the slightly burnt spinach casserole. I also had some apple cider and a blueberry muffin. The muffin was a couple days old and past its prime. As a result it crumbled too easily. I finished eating and headed to Bob's.

On the way I stopped at Moon Dancers, a local liquor store, to pick up a six pack of beer. I found a type of beer I had never tried before called Witches' Brew. It looked pretty good. It also fit in well with the whole day's theme.

As I headed to Bob's house, "Black Magic Woman" was playing on the oldies station. It seemed like a creepy coincidence. Not to mention that I am always offended when I recognize songs on the oldies station. "Black Magic Woman," was a Santana song from 1970 and might be a legitimate oldie, but the station would often include songs from the 1980s and 1990s. As far as I am concerned, if it came out during my lifetime, it is not an oldie.

CHAPTER SEVEN

~~~

W HEN I GOT to Bob's house, I was surprised to see it so tidy. I handed Bob the beer and sat down on his large leather sofa in front of his impressive sixty-inch television.

"Dude, did you clean up for me?" I asked.

"Don't flatter yourself. Remember, I had a date with Heather before the whole hair thing."

"I don't think I've met her."

"No," he said, joining me on the couch. "I only went out with her once. I kind of liked her, but I don't think it is a good sign if you break a date for hair care."

"No, sorry. I am sure she's not good for you, anyway."

"Yeah, I bet Heather drop-kicks puppies and stomps on baby chicks."

"You dodged a bullet."

Bob got up off the couch and went into the kitchen. He came back with two large bowls, one containing popcorn and the other, pretzels. He used the remote to queue up *Children of the Corn*. *Children of the Corn* is a movie from the 1980s about children who kill off the adults in a small town to serve an evil entity that lives in a cornfield. We watched in relative silence. I had forgotten that the woman from *The Terminator* movie was one of the stars. After that Bob played *The Craft*, which is about four high school students engaged in witchcraft. Three of the girls let the power go to their heads and try to kill the fourth girl.

"Do you think the people in the village we visited today pray to Manon?" I asked.

"No, I think that was made up for the movie," Bob said.

"What do witches believe in?"

Bob threw up his hands. "Why are you asking me? How would I know? Maybe I should call Heather and ask her. What a witch she is! A hundred years ago they used to burn witches like her."

"Still bitter about the date? Let it go," I said.

"I already have. I'm over it. I just feel so used. I hate it when you think things are going well and then you get blown off."

"Do you know anything about witches?" I asked.

"Just what I've learned from television and the movies," Bob said through a mouthful of popcorn. "If it helps, I have seen a lot of episodes of *Charmed* since they put it on Netflix."

"What has that taught you?"

"Mostly that witches are really hot looking and wear skimpy outfits to fight demons."

"Damn, no wonder we almost died fighting that demon last year. I didn't know there were special outfits."

"It's not just the outfits," Bob said, "you also have to look good in the outfits. Knowing magic helps too."

I shook my head. "There's always a catch."

Bob offered me more popcorn, but I refused. "Sorry about the fortune teller," he said. "I thought it would be fun. She has never freaked out like that during any of Crystal's readings."

"I wonder if I should be worried," I said, sitting up a little straighter on the couch. "It's a little like going to the doctor with a cut and having him look at it and barf."

"That's a bit of an overstatement."

"Why? She looked into my future and got sick."

"So you believe she can tell the future?" Bob said, finishing off his beer.

I hesitated just a second before saying, "No."

"Then don't worry about it." He shrugged.

"I know you're right, but a part of me wonders. We have seen some crazy stuff in the past. Maybe people *can* tell the future."

"Come on," he said, "if she could really tell the future, she would be at the racetrack making far more money than reading peoples fortunes."

"You're right. Yet, if you don't believe, why did you take me there?"

"It's fun, the tea is good, and she is really attractive."

"Yeah, I guess I'm just tired. I'm going to head home. Next time we will do this at my new pad."

"Cool."

It was late, and by the time I got home, I was exhausted. I got undressed and brushed my teeth. I was ready to forget about witches and fortune tellers. Bob's words would have been more reassuring if I hadn't had that dream—the dream I'd meant to tell him about. Hell, I couldn't tell him about the dream after his date canceled. Since my dreams have a way of leading to bad things, I was better off keeping it to myself.

Chapter Eight

~~~

I WOKE LATE. It was Sunday and I didn't have to be anywhere. I had planned to have a lazy breakfast at home and then rake leaves. From my backyard I could see that cars had already filled the orchard's parking lot. Children and their parents were drinking cider and searching for the perfect pumpkin.

I tried, but I couldn't get my mind off the strange village of witches and the even stranger fortune teller. I decided to Google witches and Wiccans to see what I could find out. There was plenty of information.

I found information on Wikipedia but was surprised to discover that there was a Wiccanpedia as well. I learned that Wicca is a modern pagan religion founded in England in the 1950s. It uses witchcraft and encompasses different customs from older religions and traditions. There is no one book they adhere to or one god. Many Wiccans believe in two gods, one male—a horned god—and one female—a moon goddess. Others believe in many gods.

Some Wiccans think of nature itself as a deity and that everything around us holds magic within it. Kind of like The Force in *Star Wars*. Rituals, the elements, and witchcraft seem to be embraced by all Wiccans and Witches.

There may be even more denominations of Wiccans than

there are Christians and Jews. They can be polytheistic, duotheistic, monotheistic, pantheistic, and atheistic. In other words—many gods, two gods, one god, god is in everything, no gods at all.

Witches are even more difficult to pin down than Wiccans. It is likely witchcraft and witches have been around since before the written word. Although the choices of deities change, most witches have close ties to nature. Also, most Witches and Wiccans seem to abide by certain rules of conduct. These include not using magic to harm others. Traditionally, good magic will come back to reward its practitioners and bad magic will come back to harm them.

I don't know why I felt drawn to look into this further. I was done with Witches and Wiccans. I now needed to get rid of leaves. I put on my jacket and gloves and headed outside to rake.

I had amassed a good pile when my neighbor pulled into his driveway in his camo-colored Chevy pickup. He removed a tarp to reveal a large and very dead buck.

He called over to me, "Let me know if you want some venison."

"Thanks," I said, "and nice buck."

"Yeah, eleven points, and I brought him down with one arrow."

"Good shot."

"Thanks."

I watched as he put a plastic sheet around it, lifted the heavy deer onto his shoulders, and carried it into his garage. He had field-dressed it, but blood remained and trickled onto the cement of his driveway. I'm not a vegetarian and in fact like venison, yet the sight of the blood made me a little sick.

At around noon I decided to take a break. I was going to head inside when a mint-green Volkswagen Beetle with daisy wheels pulled into the parking lot. I was surprised to see two of the women from the witches' village—Wendy and Alice—get out of the car. Wendy looked concerned. She wore her hair tied back in a ponytail and a simple black linen dress in contrast to the gauzy outfit from yesterday. In her store, Wendy seemed young and attractive, almost peppy. Now she looked ten years older. I noticed lines around her mouth and eyes I had not seen previously.

Alice did not want to be here at all. She wore a simple cotton blue dress with a white shirt and high collar. Her demeanor seemed severe but that had been my impression at her store as well.

"It's important that we speak with you," Wendy said as she walked toward me.

"How did you even know where I live?" I asked.

Alice walked around the car and stood behind Wendy. She was clearly uncomfortable. At the same time her stern look made me realize she also felt the situation was dire.

"You will excuse me if I don't invite you in and offer you scones and tea," I said. "I don't know anything about you, other than that you claim to be witches and live in the middle of nowhere."

"Forget the scones and tea, but you must invite us in … unless you want to talk about it in the driveway," Wendy said, her eyes narrowing.

"What if I don't want to speak with you at all?"

"I understand. We are complete strangers. I hope you understand that we would not be here if it was not a matter of life and death."

"Isn't that a bit dramatic?"

"No," she replied too quickly.

"Fine," I threw up my hands, "come in."

We walked back into the house and Wendy and Alice had a seat on the sofa in my sunken living room. I walked into the kitchen and grabbed a bottle of water from the refrigerator. I did not offer anything to my guests. I wasn't sure why I was being so rude, but the whole situation seemed ludicrous, and

I did *not* want to get involved in another supernatural mess.

"So what is so important that you found the need to follow me home? Wait, let me guess, your sister got struck down by a flying house."

"Look, he is just an ass," Alice said, speaking for the first time. "Let's get out of here."

"Bridget does not make mistakes. We have to try," Wendy told Alice.

"Fine, just get on with it," I said.

"Bridget has been accused of the worst type of magic, including murder and growing Blood Thorns. She needs a lawyer."

"Are you in Coles or Douglas County?" I asked.

"She isn't being charged with a crime under the laws of the State. She is being accused of acts against the coven."

"Then she needs a Warlock or Witch attorney who knows the rules of evidence created by the coven," I said. "Better yet, can't she just move to another coven and avoid the whole thing?"

"I told you this was a waste of time," Alice said.

"They will burn her alive if she is found guilty," Wendy said.

"Then call the police. Illinois does not put people to death anymore. We haven't since Governor Ryan issued a moratorium on the death penalty before he went to prison himself. Governor Quinn signed a bill in 2011 putting an end to it. They can't kill someone for a crime."

"The State won't put her to death; the coven will. Bridget would prefer death to telling the police or leaving the coven. All she wants to do is talk with you," Wendy said.

"Why me?" I asked.

Sitting on the edge of the couch, Wendy said, "She said when you touched she had a premonition. She also said that you felt something as well. She couldn't tell me what she saw other than that you were part of it. All she wants is for you to see her. If, after speaking with her, you don't want to take her case, then don't. She also wanted me to tell you that if you search your spirit, your heart, and your dreams, you will come."

"Why can't she come to see me?"

"The coven has restricted her movements until the trial."

"The trial?"

"October twenty-ninth and thirtieth, the day before Samhain."

"How can I prepare for a murder trial in a couple of days? I will talk to her but only to tell her in person I'm not interested."

"When will you come?" Wendy said.

"I will be there either tonight or tomorrow morning," I said.

"Thank you. She will die without your help," Wendy said.

Wendy and Alice got up in unison and headed toward the door. Both seemed deadly serious, yet I didn't believe what they'd told me could possibly be true. People did not burn witches anymore. I had little doubt they believed it, however.

I showered and put on a clean gray T-shirt and black shorts. I looked in the mirror. Was it possible? I looked older than I had an hour before. My short brown hair was grayer on the sides. I definitely needed a shave. I pulled out a razor from the medicine cabinet.

I am not what I would call particularly handsome. I lack the high cheekbones and piercing eyes of your average movie star. At the same time I am not unappealing. I still maintain a youthful appearance despite no longer being in my twenties. I am in 'decent' shape. I can run a mile or two without my heart seizing up. Although I would rather do this with a defibrillator nearby.

I decided to visit the fortune teller tomorrow after work. I figured there was no need to call ahead since she wasn't allowed to go anywhere. That and no one gave me her telephone number.

I sat down to watch television. Yet for some reason I couldn't stop thinking about the fortune teller. She was attractive and mysterious and obviously as crazy as a howler monkey hopped up on Red Bull, but it was hard to get her out of my head.

After a half hour I gave up on trying to do nothing. If I couldn't stop thinking about her, I might as well go see her. The whole damn thing was crazy. This was not Salem in the 1600s. We didn't have witch trials. I couldn't help but think it was all a practical joke.

CHAPTER NINE

~~~

I LEFT THE house as the sun was starting to set. I hoped I
could remember how to get to the witches' village. I knew I
could call Bob if necessary. Not only didn't I have a telephone
number for Bridget, but I didn't recall seeing a telephone in
her house. I assumed witches were allowed to have cellphones.
How else would her clients get in touch with her?

Oddly, I didn't get lost. Since I often get lost going to the
supermarket, this was no minor feat.

When I pulled up into her driveway, I saw that the front
porch was lit with a blue bulb, giving the white paint a bluish
cast. White candles at least two feet tall were lit in the windows
in front.

I walked up the porch stairs and was about to knock when
the front door opened on its own. Bridget Gillis, the fortune
teller, stood ten feet away. So who had opened the door? I
looked around but saw only Bridget, and then pretty much all
other thoughts flew out of my head. She was like something
out of a bondage fantasy in her black leather pants and corset
top. Her already piercing blue eyes were accentuated by dark
makeup. Her lips were painted cherry red. The house smelled
as though someone had been burning sage.

"Am I here at a bad time? You look like you're going out," I said.

"I was waiting for you. Thank you so much for coming. I wouldn't bother you if it wasn't a matter of life and death."

"So I've been told."

"Follow me and I'll explain everything. It's a long story."

"I can't image how I can help you, but I will hear you out," I said as I followed behind her, trying not to stare at her leather-clad behind.

She led me back to the room where we did the Tarot reading and through the back door. We crossed a hallway into a large kitchen. The portion of the house open to the public was mostly furnished and decorated with Victorian antiques and collectables. So the modern kitchen was a strange contrast. The kitchen had white granite countertops and cherry wood cabinets. The appliances were modern and stainless steel. There were watercolor paintings on the walls of flowers and vegetables. She gestured toward an Ikea maple table, so I took a seat as she put on a kettle for tea.

"I do not expect you to understand or accept what I am going to tell you," she said, "but I do pray that you'll hear me out." The fortune teller's tone and demeanor were so serious that they seemed disharmonious with her sexy attire.

"My family originally came from England. Nineteenth century England was supposed to be an enlightened time, a time when people would no longer be ruled by superstition. Witches were no longer considered a threat. Except that they were. Maybe there were no witch trials, but it was not safe. That is why my great-great aunt, Bridget Bishop, decided to move to America. To find land in the middle of nowhere and create a village of witches where people could openly practice their craft."

"Your great-great aunt sounds like an adventurous lady for the time," I said.

"Yes, I was named after her and this is her house. It took a long time for her to find this area, but when she did, she knew it would be our home."

"So, with the discrimination of the old country behind her, she built this community," I said.

"Not quite," Bridget said, leaning against the granite countertop. It was difficult not to become mesmerized by her movements, so I kept looking away, trying to concentrate on what she was saying. "She married the richest man in the area," Bridget continued, "and was accused of casting a love spell to enchant him."

"Was he a witch ... or is it warlock?"

"No, nothing like that." She waved her long fingers in denial. "Just a wealthy farmer. He was a widower and had six children. All of them were furious that he gave half his estate to my aunt after his death. That estate included the land this house rests on, the village, and an additional hundred acres."

The kettle whistled and Bridget poured the tea. She placed a bone china cup in front of me and added to the saucer some chocolate cookies with a raspberry glaze.

"So what happened?" Suddenly hungry, I took a bite of the delicious cookie.

"There was a fight in court over the estate, but my aunt prevailed. The marriage had lasted ten years. It would have been hard to convince a court he had been bewitched for so long.

"So she created this community. She had the first five houses built to her specifications. I still have the plans in the attic. All of it was drawn up by hand ... no computers back then. This house and the four others remain standing to this day. The families of the original settlers continue to live in those homes. My aunt claimed there was magical significance to the placement of the homes and wanted powerful witches to live there. So it was agreed that as long as descendants of the original settlers lived in the homes, then they could stay there, rent free. The other houses and stores came later."

"That seems like an interesting estate."

"As a lawyer you must know a lot about such things."

"No, I don't do estate planning. I didn't even take 'stiffs and gifts' in law school."

" 'Stiffs and gifts'?"

"Sort of a nickname for estate planning." I took a sip of tea. "I gather this story is related to your situation," I said. The tea sent a surge of warmth through my body like a hot toddy.

"Yes, there are conditions associated with our living in the community and benefiting from the land. My aunt was afraid of our Amish and Christian neighbors. She felt that if black magic or human sacrifice were ever to come to light, then witches would be burned once again. Certain spells are forbidden."

"You are being accused of casting forbidden spells?"

She sighed and sat down next to me. "Yes, the worst of the worst. I am accused of growing Blood Thorns."

I wondered what the heck a Blood Thorn was. "The punishment for growing 'Blood Thorns' is excommunication?"

"No," she said, tapping her red-lacquered fingernails on the table, "death by fire. Then my house would go to the coven."

I watched her nails drumming on the table. "Seems like an overreaction to strange gardening habits … no matter how bad Blood Thorns are," I said.

She put her hands in her lap and said, "Blood Thorns are a plant that feeds on human blood. The blood of children. They grow a single fruit. It looks like one of those Korean melons but is blood red in color. It is said that an evil witch can obtain unthinkable power by ingesting one at the witching hour on *All Hallow's Eve*."

"How do you know so much about it?" I said.

"My aunt's library is quite extensive. I know all about black magic, but I choose not to use it. Witchcraft is like the Indian idea of karma. Bad magic will come back to harm its master just as good magic will provide greater rewards."

I cleared my throat. I was uncomfortable with this whole situation. "You do realize I can't represent you. I don't know anything about your customs and laws."

"When I read your fortune, I had just finished reading my own. The cards I gave to you were meant for me, thus they were in the reverse order and the reverse position. The result was far worse. The Tower and the Ten of Swords represented my future. That was the fifth deck in a row that produced identical cards. When we touched I had a premonition that you would stand before the elders with me. I also felt that you were my only hope."

"It was just a daydream," I said gently. I wished I could help her, but it was impossible.

She shook her head vehemently. "No, it wasn't and you know that as well. You felt something. You saw me in your dreams."

"I am not a witch," I said.

"No but you have premonitions. You may not recognize them or understand them but you do have them. They haunt your dreams and make you a beacon for magical forces. Come with me. I'd like to show you something." She took my hand in hers and began to lead me out of the kitchen and down the hallway toward a staircase.

Her touch sent ripples of warmth through my body, and her scent grew stronger as we walked together. I took a deep whiff of sandalwood, anise, and cloves. I could actually feel the warmth emanating from her body.

We walked up the back stairs to the second level of the home. From there we walked down a hallway to the end, where a door opened up to reveal a smaller, narrower staircase. This led to a library. Oak bookshelves lined the walls, with an oil painting separating each shelf. The room smelled of old leather.

There was an antique tiger oak library table and four maroon leather club chairs around it. A wooden podium against one wall looked like it had come from a church. In addition there was a ladder on wheels that moved along a track. The ladder was necessary because books were shelved all the way to the top of the twelve-foot ceiling.

"Mr. Levi once offered me over a hundred thousand dollars for these books. Many have been in my family since the seventeenth century. They are beyond priceless. The collection includes the grimoire of my great-great aunt. Their pages reveal some of the greatest mysteries of magic. Mostly good magic."

The paintings on the wall were all of stoic looking women in conservative attire. Although the pictures were well rendered, the models appeared lifeless. Only one image broke the mold. It was a picture of my hostess lying naked on her back, surrounded by lit candles. She was in the middle of a pentacle painted in red. The painting was erotic and out of place in this room. It reminded me of a heavy metal album cover. She wore the same silver necklace she was wearing this evening.

"I must say the painting of you is a lot different than the others," I said. "I would have liked to see you model for it." I blushed. I had spoken my thoughts aloud. She hadn't invited me here to seduce me.

"That is not me," she said. "Look at the date."

I took a closer look at the canvas. The piece was signed by John William Waterhouse. The date was clearer than the signature: 1874. It was not possible, of course.

"That is my great-great aunt, Bridget Bishop. We do look alike."

"The necklace is the same," I said.

"It was hers."

"Your aunt was lovely."

Then Bridget did something totally unexpected. She kissed me gently on the lips. Passion rushed through me and I kissed her back. I was almost feverish with desire, and it scared me. It had been a long time since I had been with a woman romantically. Susan and I had broken up over a year ago. Yet what I felt now was more than desperation; it was a longing so intense that it completely overwhelmed me.

Bridget opened the door to a round room—the house's turret. The ceiling was painted dark blue and the walls a deep maroon. Lit candles were placed at random intervals throughout the room. The bed was covered with a blood-red velvet spread. Bridget removed her shoes and sat in the middle of the bed as she slowly untied the tight corset and slid the leather pants down over her legs. Impossibly, she had the same tattoos as in my dream, the suits from the Tarot. Her body was perfection. Her large breasts were firm and her hips and stomach strong like an athlete's.

I didn't realize I was next to her until she began to undress me. The depth of my longing caused tears to drip down my face, and she held me close. The sweat of our bodies mingled as we made love. The parts of my body that did not have direct contact with her felt jealous of those that did. I could still feel the heat coming from her in waves. Even as we were making love, it was not enough. I wanted to be a part of her, to disappear into her. I refused to let her go, even when we were done. I continued holding on to her until we both fell asleep.

I AWOKE AS Bridget was getting out of bed. Her long black hair ran down past her hips. She turned to me, unashamed of her nakedness. Not that there was anything to be ashamed of. In any case, she certainly wasn't shy.

It was Monday morning but I had nothing urgent at work. Still ....

Suddenly I realized what was going on. "You planned this," I said. "You needed me to fall in love with you so I would help with your case."

"You were already in love with me," she responded.

"Do you love me?" I said, hearing the vulnerability in my voice and not liking it.

"Does it matter?"

"Of course."

"Then I love you," she said simply.

"You say that in the same manner as one would say they love an apple," I said. In answer she bent over and gave me a soft kiss on the cheek.

"I love apples too. Magic is in you as well as in an apple."

"That's why you dressed so provocatively. I think you were trying to seduce me, Mrs. Robinson."

She smiled. "I'm glad it worked, and it is Ms. Gillis," she said, "not Mrs. Robinson. I know not of this person you speak of. I would hope that whether or not we made love, you would not allow me to die for a crime I had no part in."

"Lawyers are not allowed to have sex with their clients," I said.

"You will not be my lawyer. You will simply be my advocate before the counsel. You will help me find the evil witch or warlock who did this."

"How do you know anyone did this?" I said, holding my hands out, palm up. "Maybe the whole thing is fabricated."

"No, they could not get this far based on an accusation alone. Something happened; I just didn't do it."

"It's not worth the risk of dying to go through with this," I insisted. "Give up the house and move. Do you really want to live in a community where one of its members would kill a child to cultivate 'Blood Thorns'?"

"I do not expect you to understand. I will die before I leave my coven."

"Come back to bed," I said. "I have things I want to do to you."

"No time," she said. "My trial begins at nine a.m. on October twenty-ninth. Today is the twenty-seventh. That gives us two days to prepare. Alice and Wendy will be here in an hour."

I stood up and began looking for my clothes. "I want Bob to help as well. We work well together and our time is limited."

"Whatever you think," she said, handing me my boxer shorts.

"I think you should come back to bed and ravage me," I said.

"I meant as it relates to my defense," she said, looking

through her closet. "I'll meet you downstairs. I'm making breakfast. Wendy and Alice will bring the supplies, and I have a couple of books you will need to read."

She slipped on a simple cotton dress and tied her hair back into a ponytail.

"Get dressed," she said, indicating the rest of my clothes on a chair. "There is a bathroom on the second floor landing next to the door you will go through at the base of the stairwell." She spoke with no affect, as though she were a stewardess giving instructions as to what to do in case of a water landing during a flight from Chicago to Las Vegas.

She opened the door and left the room. The black cat I'd seen on my first visit entered the room. The beast jumped onto the bed and gave me a mischievous stare. His fur was short and looked slick. I prefer the fluffier variety of cats. I suspect that he preferred a different type of human as well.

I retrieved my cellphone from my pants and looked through the calendar. For the next twenty minutes I made phone calls and rearranged my schedule. I would not be back at work until after Halloween.

CHAPTER TEN

~~~

I DIALED BOB's telephone number. He picked up on the sixth ring.

"Do you have any idea what time it is?" Bob sounded tired and annoyed.

"Yes."

"Well, what time is it?"

"Nine twenty."

Bob's voice rose. "In the morning?" he said.

"Yes."

"Why the hell are you calling at such a ridiculous time?"

"I need your help."

"I assume that means that you're either in the hospital or better yet in bed with two gorgeous women and feel you can only satisfy one of them."

"No, it's a legal thing," I said. "No, that's not right, sort of a supernatural-witch-coven-tribunal thing."

"You have gone completely nuts."

"Look, it may truly be a matter of life and death. Bring your van and computer equipment to the fortune teller's house and I will explain it all."

He paused, possibly in shock. Finally he said, "I never thought I would hear you say those words in my lifetime. Fine,

I will be there in an hour. By the way, you owe me a favor."

I went to the second floor landing. The bathroom was all white with a fluffy white towel on a chrome rack. I showered and wrapped the towel around me before heading back upstairs to put on my clothes from the night before. I retraced my steps and returned to the kitchen on the ground level.

Bridget was cooking eggs, sausages, and potatoes. She pointed to a large room off the kitchen—a combination dining room and family room. Wendy and Alice were sitting at the large Amish-made oak dining room table. I took a seat. I assumed the kitchen table was reserved for less serious matters. Neither of them seemed surprised to see me.

"Bob will be here in an hour," I said in a voice loud enough to be heard in the kitchen.

"Good," Bridget said through the kitchen entrance.

"All right, where do we start?" Wendy asked, looking at me for guidance.

"Don't look at me," I said. "I'm not the leader of this group."

"Bridget said we were going to help you with the investigation," Wendy said.

Bridget walked into the room carrying a large platter filled with food.

"Yes, that is what I said," Bridget said.

"Fine," I said, counting on my fingers. "I need a copy of the charges, the discovery, and the rules."

"There are no written charges," Bridget said. She walked over to a bookshelf in the back of the room and scanned it as she added, "We will meet at the Witching Hour with the elders."

"The Witching Hour … midnight?" I asked.

"The Witching Hour can be either noon or midnight. In this case, noon." Bridget found what she was looking for and brought the thin leather book back to the table. "This book will explain the laws of the coven. It spells out to some degree the procedural rules. The triers of fact are three elders. You have met Raymond Levi; he will be presenting the case against me.

He is also an elder but will not vote on the verdict. He will let you know more about the accusations."

"You mean the snarky dude at the book store. He already dislikes Bob and me."

"He will be fair," Bridget said.

"I hope so. Your life depends on it."

"Our system of laws has worked for thousands of years. It is not an adversary process like American law. It is based on respect and tradition."

"Yes, the death penalty is certainly civilized. Burning witches is the very height of civility."

Bridget frowned and pounded the table once with her small fist. "You know nothing of our ways. Please respect our traditions," she said.

I folded my arms across my chest. "You invited me to this shindig, not the other way around."

We sat in silence after that. I couldn't explain my feelings. I was in love with Bridget yet hated her at the same time. Wendy and Alice treated her with reverence and were clearly shocked by my lack of respect. I decided to concentrate on my food. It was good if not exciting. When I finished, Bridget got up to take my plate.

"Why don't we clean up in here while you read the book I just handed you? There is a door to your left that will take you into the waiting area by the front door. You can wait for Bob as you get acquainted with the edicts passed down by my great-great aunt, which have been followed by our people ever since."

I did as I was told. I returned to the front entrance area of the house, the one with the fireplace, and sat on the velvet sofa. It would be hard to concentrate on reading with Bridget around. Everything about her confused me. She was not at all my type. Yet at the same time I loved her. Rather than try and sort out my feelings, I got to work.

The book in my hand was thin, less than twenty pages.

The tooled leather cover was branded with a pentagram. The lines of the symbol were designed to look like branches. The pages themselves were parchment that appeared to be made of deerskin with a slightly red tinge. I wasn't sure how I knew this, since I'd never seen deerskin parchment before. The writing was an overly ornate calligraphy irregular enough that they could only have been rendered by hand. There were scribbled notes next to certain passages; some of these were crude sketches.

The first page had the name Bridget Bishop written in ornate letters with a sapling under four silver moons in progressive stages from a new moon, to a crescent moon, to a gibbous and finally the full moon. The outline of the sapling had an almost-human shape.

The next page was written in calligraphy and did not have a heading.

> The purpose and design of this community is to live at peace with nature, our neighbors, and the larger community. This coven has joined together witches of different faiths and we live as one. We have left the old world because witchcraft and magic will never be accepted there. That is despite the claims of kings and queens that this is a time of enlightenment. We will only be safe nestled among nothingness in the middle of the vastness of America. Even there we will be at risk if our community extends itself.
>
> Whether it is Salem in America or The Great Witch Craze of Europe, no place is safe. This text shall state the resolutions of this community. Its purpose is to allow our people to live in peace.
>
> Dark magic has its own sanctions from the ancient spirits, gods, and nature herself. Black magic always comes at a price. However, it is not for me to put a value on the soul. Yet, black magic may stir the embers of hate and

renew the blood lust against our kind. Thus, this coven is barred now and forever from performing the blood sins and spells listed in this text or the rituals outlined. The punishment for a violation is death by fire. The burning of the flesh will take place at the Witching Hour of the next Sabbat after the coven's judgment.

I got up and walked around. I kept the book in my hand, allowing my thumb to keep my place. I was completely out of my depth. Sitting down again, I flipped the page.

The next page had the Roman numeral I and then BLOOD THORNS written in block letters across the top. Below was a sketch with a thorn bush. The bush had few leaves and large thorns. The twisted branches looked thick, like the rope of a great ship. The most disturbing part of the image was the single fruit that hung down. It looked like a small melon but was shaped like a baby in the fetal position.

The next page bore the Roman numeral II and then BLOOD SACRIFICE. This was followed by the image of a cutting board made into a table. A cleaver and a small heart lay atop the board. The table was at a slight angle, allowing the blood to pour down into a metal bucket.

The following page, labeled Roman numeral III, was called LOVE SPELLS OF BLOOD. The image showed an arm: a large hand was squeezing a human heart; blood dripped down its wrist.

This page was followed by another that had the Roman numeral IV and then BLOOD CURSES. The sketch depicted dead crops and a dead cow. Blood was spilled on the ground beneath the crops and the animal.

The next page, Roman numeral V, was called BLOOD BATH. The image showed a large trough used for watering horses. The tub was filled with blood and floating human body parts. It seemed to be set up for a satanic game of bobbing for apples.

Roman numeral VI was named RAISING THE DEAD

(NECROMANCY). There was a sketch of a coffin with smoke rising from it. The smoke coalesced in the air to form a human face. This image had writing below:

> The dead must never be molested, whether to bring back the flesh or the spirit. A séance is forbidden, just as is raising the flesh itself.

The next page had the Roman numeral VII and the words BLOOD GLAMOUR. The passage read:

> A glamour is a creative and fun spell used to create an illusion. It is amusing to change one's hair color or outfit with a simple spell. Yet, a Blood Glamour is forbidden. There are two types of blood glamours: the first conceals danger in order to cause death. The illusion of a bridge over a canyon can cause a person to fall to their death. A permanent or long-term glamour is also considered a blood glamour and is therefore forbidden. To make oneself look young to attract a mate and to continue the illusion over time is not allowed. A permanent glamour requires the blood of an innocent to perform. A fleeting glamour does not.

I heard a bell and looked up to see Bob through the glass of the front door. I let him in. He carried a messenger bag that I assumed contained a laptop and was wearing pajama bottoms and a Black Sabbath concert T-shirt with the image of a winged succubus on the front. His hair was curly and appeared unwashed and his goatee needed a trim.

"This better be fucking good to get me out of bed," he said.

"What, no 'hello, good to see you'?"

"Not until I get a coffee and a reasonable explanation as to why I am here."

Just as I was about to respond, Bridget entered the room with a large silver tray that held two porcelain cups and an insulated pitcher of coffee. There was also a basket filled with muffins and cinnamon rolls. The room instantly filled with the scent of warm rolls and cinnamon. She put the tray down on a small table, then went over to Bob and gave him a lingering hug. For moment I was gripped with jealousy, but it soon passed.

"I will get you some eggs and sausages and be back in a moment," Bridget said, leaving the room.

"So, are you going to tell me what's going on?" asked Bob, mollified by the hug and warm rolls.

I gave Bob the short version of what happened, starting with the dream. I skipped the part where I slept with Bridget. He listened intently but I could tell by the look on his face he thought I was crazy. Bridget entered the room with a plate full of eggs and sausages and left us to our conversation.

We both took a seat on the maroon couch.

"What are we being paid?" Bob asked.

"I will pay you for your time," I said.

"What are you being paid?"

"Why do you care?"

"Because I am thinking, based on the way you looked at Bridget when she came in the room and on the fact that a sane person wouldn't get involved in this mess, that you have gone beyond the fortune teller-client relationship."

"Does it matter? We can't allow the woman I love to be roasted like a marshmallow at a Boy Scout jamboree."

" 'The woman you love'? You have known her a couple of days. It took you a couple of years to admit you loved Susan. It took you three months to decide if you loved the last limited edition Pop-Tarts. By the time you decided, they'd stopped making them."

I shrugged. "Maybe I'm over my fear of commitment."

"Maybe you have been repressing your feelings for so long that when a sexy witch shows you some attention you blow the whole thing out of proportion."

I finished another cup of coffee, although the caffeine was starting to make me jittery. "I thought you would be happy for me. You're the one who has been hounding me to find a girlfriend. In fact you went on and on about how 'hot' she is. Is this about jealousy?"

Bob looked hurt. "Dude," he implored, "I want you to be happy. Just be careful."

"Maybe she is too good-looking for me. Is that it? A truly good-looking woman couldn't be interested in me?"

"Mellow out," he said, waving his hands in the air. "I'm not saying that at all. Well, she *is* a lot better looking than you. But good-looking women date ugly guys all the time. Lyle Lovett was married to Julia Roberts."

"Gee, thanks ... and fuck you very much. Are you going to help me are not?"

"Of course I will help. I am just saying, be careful. Try and stay objective."

I knew I was being unreasonably defensive. "Even if I didn't have feelings for Bridget, I couldn't let anyone die if I could help. It's the right thing to do."

I knew Bob was fully focused on our conversation, because so far his breakfast was untouched.

"We don't even have the death penalty in Illinois," he said. "Why doesn't she just move out of the village and live somewhere safe where crazy laws don't apply?"

"She would rather die than leave the coven."

"I don't believe this anyway," he said. "Are you sure it's not some kind of prank?"

"I don't know what to believe," I admitted. "We have to go to the witch meeting place at noon. Why don't you eat while I skim through this book?"

CHAPTER ELEVEN

～～～

Bridget entered the room just as I began going through the book once again. She asked Bob to come with her, leaving me with this strange text for company. I noticed that Bob still had not eaten anything.

The next section in Bridget Bishop's grimoire dealt with holidays, ceremonies, and rituals. She referred to the traditional holidays as Sabbats. The first holiday listed was Samhain, known to us as Halloween. The coven was instructed to leave out food in the center of the village and decorate with hollowed-out pumpkins and turnips. At this time of the year, the veil between the living and the dead would be at its thinnest. If the dead wished to cross into the world of the living, Samhain was their best opportunity. There were other Sabbats, of course, but I figured I'd better stick to the relevant parts of the book.

Bridget's list of approved holidays, ceremonies, and rituals to be celebrated was followed by another list, this one of forbidden holidays, ceremonies, and rituals. This included bastardized versions of holidays from the first list. Satanhain called for blood sacrifice. Blood would be placed in a pie pan before the door of the home to draw forth ghosts and demons from the netherworld. After being exposed to the spirits, the blood acquired strange, magical qualities. Many of the other holidays also had twisted versions that required dark prayers and the drawing of blood.

The Christian holidays had bastardized versions as well. When I was in Israel a professor told me about the Black Mass, a satanic ritual similar to a traditional Catholic Mass but turning it on its head. Christmas's dark equivalent was the Malum Mass, which involved feasting on animal blood. A dead tree would be stripped of its leaves and animal entrails used to decorate the empty branches. Easter had a perverted version where a witch could attempt to raise the dead. Apparently, it was not uncommon for the dead to be adversely transformed. The book goes on to explain that spirits of the dead tend to be ethereal or partially transparent.

My study was interrupted by the entrance of Bob, Alice, Wendy, and Bridget. Bob was wearing linen pants and a white, loose-fitting shirt.

"It is after eleven and I want to get there early," Bridget said.

I had no idea how time had gone by so quickly. I still had not finished the book and did not understand the procedure for this "trial." I was also a bit confused by Bob's wardrobe upgrade.

"Why the change of clothes?" I asked Bob as I got to my feet.

"Apparently witches don't like Black Sabbath," he said. "Who knew?"

I tried to remember if that was a forbidden holiday on my list. If not, the T-shirt still seemed in bad form. I wondered if I should change as well.

"Should I change?" I asked.

"No time," Bridget said. "Everyone out."

We walked around the back, where houses lined both sides of a grassy park-like area about the length of two football fields. There was a large fire pit near the middle of the park, flanked by two unpainted wood gazebos. There were no trees in this area and it seemed a bit bare.

"That building at the very end is used as the village's gathering place," Bridget said, "sort of the village hall. You can see the two lanterns on the front porch have been lit. They are to let the coven know of the meeting."

The building was one-story high with a porch in front. It was painted white with green shingles. Lanterns hung from plant hooks on either side of the door, as Bridget had described. From this distance, the flames appeared to be bluish green. I thought they might be gas. Others in the community were heading in the same direction. As we got closer to the building, I noticed a pole with a cast-iron hook in the shape of a crescent moon and a large brass bell with a rope hanging from the top of the moon. An antique dinner bell or school bell, perhaps.

When we entered the building there were already close to fifty people in attendance. The interior was constructed of unpainted pine boards, and the roof bracing was visible with no insulation to obscure the arch of the ceiling. It reminded me of a simple church or a one-room schoolhouse. At the back of the room was a stage a foot higher than the floor. A wooden table perhaps fifteen feet long sat upon the stage. On the table were five hour glasses in different sizes, a large crystal, four thin books, and two larger books. The books all looked old and official.

A stern-looking man and two women were sitting behind the table. The man—fiftyish, bald, and beardless—wore a black suit and a white button-down shirt with no tie. Both women had gray hair and both wore simple cotton dresses—one gray with a white collar and the other black. The first wore her hair short, the other, long. The short-haired one, who also wore glasses, looked older and appeared to be in charge, especially since she sat between the other two.

Bridget led us to a bench centered directly in front of the stage. The other benches were lined up on each side of the room and separated by a walkway. The five of us took our seats.

We waited for ten minutes in silence as people from the

village filled the seats behind us. There was quiet murmuring and the sound of sparse movement behind us as the gathering crowd tried to remain still. The woman with the short gray hair broke the silence.

"Who are these people you have brought?" she said, pointing directly at Bob and me.

"My advocates," Bridget said, rising to her feet.

"They are not of this coven. They do not appear to share our faith," the woman said.

"Our faith, based on the mandates of the coven," Bridget said.

"Yes," the woman agreed.

"Our canon dictates that an advocate is a person chosen by the accused. It does not specify a 'member of the coven' and it does not say a 'witch.' If that was the intent, our ancestors would have said so. Unless you feel they were ignorant or lacked foresight."

"The intent of our laws is to protect this village and its members from the threat of and exposure to the outside world. Bringing in outside advocates is a risk our ancestors would not have allowed."

"Then my demand for advocates of my choosing is denied."

"We will take a recess for five minutes. When we return we will rule on your request."

The three people on the stage got up and left the room. There was a door at the back that I assume led outside. The murmuring of the crowd rose as if the people were confused by the turn of events.

"Doesn't due process require counsel of your choosing?" I asked Bridget.

"That is for the elders to decide. Yet, they have never in the past ignored an edict directly from the book."

We sat in silence until the elders returned. The woman with the short gray hair looked annoyed. The crowd instantly went silent.

"You may choose your advocates, under the condition that we be allowed to cast a spell over them to bar them from speaking of these proceedings to the outside word."

"As you wish," Bridget said.

"I don't want to be spelled," Bob whispered as Wendy elbowed him in the gut.

"We will break for one hour while the ingredients are prepared for the spell." The woman with the short gray hair turned over one of the hour glasses and hit the table with the crystal. The crystal flashed with a strange purple and green light, like a spark, when it struck the table. The room emptied out, leaving only the five of us still sitting there. Bridget seemed pleased, having won a small victory, although I couldn't see how it benefited us. I would do my best as her advocate but I still felt she would be better served by someone with experience.

Bob seemed nervous. It was clear he would have preferred other advocates as well. He turned to me and whispered, "I don't want a spell cast on me."

Bridget laid a hand on his leg. "There will be no harm to you. It simply keeps you from telling the outside world about coven business."

"If I do tell the outside world, will I turn into a toad?" he asked.

"You won't be able to tell anyone so there is no risk in your being toaded," Bridget said.

"Toaded? That's not a word or a proper verb," I said.

"It is also impossible," Bob said. "A spell can't make someone unable to talk."

"If you don't think it will work, then who cares, why worry?" I said.

"Do spells have side effects? Could I turn green or get warts?" Bob asked.

Bridget kept a straight face. "Some spells have side effects. Yet, those are limited to the person who cast the spell and only as to dark magic. You will be fine."

"You're both cowards," Alice sneered.

"Shut up," Wendy told her, giving her a slap on the arm. "They're trying to help us."

We all rose to our feet and looked at one another, unsure what to do. We decided to wait around. I couldn't help but notice that even in a simple dress Bridget looked stunning. I wondered if we had a future. I supposed that would depend upon if *she* had a future. The outcome of this case was becoming more and more important to me.

The hour passed quickly and the room once again filled with villagers. A tall, stout man wearing overalls—the guy was big enough to play Frankenstein's Monster—brought in a wooden crate, carried it up to the stage, and left it on the table. From the crate he removed a small Bunsen burner and a cauldron with three metal feet to keep it from falling over. This was followed by a bottle of Evian, a Zippo lighter, and three bags of what I assumed to be herbs, a stick of some kind, a block of metal, and a knife.

When the elders entered the room, the crowd all stood. Only Bob and I remained seated. The man poured the water into the cauldron and lit the burner. In unison the elders began reciting a spell in a language I did not recognize as the short-haired woman added the three bags of herbs. She then used the knife to strip bark from the branch. She also picked up the block of metal, which looked like silver, and used the knife to add a few strips to the concoction.

"The advocates will inhale the fumes from the cauldron and read the text we have provided," the short-haired elder said.

"Shit, that is how they make meth, isn't it?" Bob whispered to me.

"It's not meth," I whispered back.

"They use metal in meth."

"They unwrap a battery to get lithium for meth. I think that was silver."

"Fine, but if I get addicted and start picking at my skin and ignoring my dental care, it is your ass I intend to blame."

We stood, walked up the stairs and onto the stage. I felt nervous staring out into the crowd. A sheet of parchment was placed on the table.

"Read the words and then breathe from the cauldron," the short-haired elder ordered.

Together Bob and I read aloud: "We may speak freely of all matters but those of the coven. Our speech mute washed away by winds—western, eastern, northern, and southern."

I felt stupid reading this silly passage but did as I was told. Bob clearly was uncomfortable as well. We both breathed from the cauldron. The air had the texture of fake fog from a concert fog machine. It smelled of the earth. I felt a little dizzy but I was not high or sick.

That's a good sign … I think went through my head.

"Let us begin," the short-haired woman said, directing us to our seats with a wave of her hand. "Bridget, would you like to introduce your advocates?"

"Yes, this is Samuel Roberts and Robert Sizemore. Neither studies the craft or engages in the use of magic."

I stood as my name was mentioned, but Bob did not. Bridget's introduction was delivered so matter-of-factly that I felt a little insulted. I guess I couldn't expect her to introduce me as the love of her life, but 'the smart and talented Mr. Roberts' would have been preferable. Even 'the powerful and distinguished Mr. Roberts.'

"May I ask why you would bring in outsiders for something so important?" the woman with the long gray hair asked.

"It was a premonition. When I touched Mr. Roberts I felt it was his role to be by my side. He is also attuned to the world of magic. I don't know how or why, but I believe he has some insight into our world."

"You know I love you, Bridget," the long-haired woman said. "But if you have committed the atrocities alleged I will see you burn." Steel was in her gaze.

"For the sake of our advocates," Short-haired Woman said, "I will make introductions. I am Glenda LeFay." To my left is Abraham Mage." Mr. Mage stood and then returned to his seat. "To my right is Agnes Moore." The other woman stood. "We will act as judges for this tribunal. Mr. Levi will present the case against Ms. Gillis."

The man we had met in the book store stood up and then sat again quickly, his movements stiff and awkward as I remembered. I hadn't noticed him in the front row of the audience. He wore dark pants, a green tweed jacket, a white shirt, a green bowtie, and wire-rimmed spectacles. I was reminded of a scholarly, unusually tall leprechaun. All he needed was a jaunty green hat.

"We are considered the elders and leaders of this community. We are not the oldest members, as you may have noticed. Being an elder is not based solely on years of life but on family lines and power. We are all direct descendants of the first settlers of this village. Mr. Levi is considered an elder but since he will be presenting the evidence he will not help determine the outcome of the case. He is, however, entitled to equal respect. Ms. Gillis is obviously not very old but her family started this village and this coven, and she is therefore considered an elder. She is entitled to respect from all of us."

She paused, so I seized my chance and stood. "Will we be provided with an opportunity to speak with the witnesses, to view the evidence and to know when this … wrongdoing allegedly took place?" I asked.

Bridget quickly rose and placed a hand on my shoulder. "You will have to excuse my advocate," she said. "He does not understand our ways. He is a lawyer in the outside world."

"I understand. Like witches, you lawyers are also feared and despised by the outside world. The difference is, for us, that reputation is undeserved," Ms. LeFay said.

I could hear stifled giggles from the villagers. If we were not here to get a copy of the allegations, a list of witnesses, and some idea of the evidence, then why were we here? How could I help with the case? I didn't even know when or where this so-called "crime" had occurred.

"I would ask that everyone cooperate with Mr. Roberts and Mr. Sizemore," Ms. LeFay said, addressing the crowd. "If they ask to speak with you, please speak honestly and freely. If they ask you to come before this tribunal, then do so. The family of Bridget Gillis was responsible for all of us being here. Her great-great aunt, Bridget Bishop, turned a dream into reality when she created this utopia. Before we cast judgment upon our sister witch, there must be no doubt as to her guilt. When it comes to defending yourself, Bridget, we are at your disposal and that of your advocates. Each member of the coven will help."

She lifted her arms to the crowd like a Baptist preacher. "We all love Bridget Gillis. Her death diminishes us all as a community and each of us as individuals. It is my sincere hope that she did not do what she is alleged to have done. If you can help in that regard you have done a service to the coven."

She lowered her voice dramatically as she continued, "At the same time, there is a reason these spells have been banned. The murder of children is abhorrent to us. The draining of a child's blood, his power, and life energy is the very definition of evil. This aberrant behavior puts all witches at risk. If a witch places individual power above the collective good of the community, then he or she must die," Ms. LeFay concluded.

"When will this proceeding commence?" Bridget asked.

"You have the rest of today and all day tomorrow to prepare. We will begin the following day, October twenty-ninth, at sunrise, and go through the thirtieth. If you are found to have committed these atrocities, you will be burned at noon on Samhain, the day you would have ingested the unholy fruit of the Blood Thorns. It is my hope that your great-great aunt will cross over to bring your soul to the afterlife."

She picked up the crystal and struck it on the table with a

thud and a spark. Apparently we were done. The crowd slowly filed out of the meeting room. Bridget and the rest of us got up and exited through the back.

As the four of us walked back to Bridget's house, the other villagers seemed to actively avoid us. I felt like I had some horrible disease or my deodorant had failed me. It could be a long few days.

"I'm going to run to my shop and pick up lunch for us," Wendy said. "I have a feeling there is no reason to stay at work. I can't imagine getting much business done until this is resolved."

"I was just thinking that," Alice responded. "I'm going to put up a closed sign and change the message on my answering machine." She and Wendy headed in the direction of their shops.

"You and Bob can stay with me," Bridget said. "I suspect you will have a lot of work to do over the next few days. At least I hope you will. My life is in your hands, after all."

"I need to head home and get some clothes," I said. "I also have a few work-related issues to take care of."

"I need to stop off at home as well," Bob said.

"Why don't we eat lunch first and plan how we are going to divide up the next day and a half before the hearing begins?" Bridget suggested.

"You should call it a trial," I said, sick and tired of all this pussyfooting around the direness of the situation, "more accurately, a *witch* trial. If the punishment for guilt is being burned at the stake, the word 'hearing' doesn't do it justice." I knew I sounded fed up, but that's exactly how I felt.

"I do need to get back," Bob insisted. "Let's eat and plan after we return. Sam, why don't we take your car? I'll get the van later."

"Fine," Bridget said, "but please don't take too long. And Bob, no concert T-shirts." She gave him a stern look.

For Bob to suggest skipping a meal or even delaying a meal

was highly irregular. Also, I thought he would have had us both take our vehicles so he could drop his beloved van off in his garage and drive back with me. Clearly he thought we had a lot to discuss.

CHAPTER TWELVE

～～

AFTER BOB AND I got into my Honda and closed the doors, Bob began speaking, even before I could turn the key. I sensed an intervention coming on. Bob grabbed the front of my shirt and said, "I have been with you every step of the way. We have battled voodoo spirits, Satan worshipping madmen, and even Ancient Egyptian gods. I have gone along with it. We had to protect the world. But this is about one person who may be guilty anyway. I have a feeling we should just walk. Leave and not come back."

"How can we?" I said helplessly. "Bridget could die!"

"Maybe she deserves to die," Bob said, letting go of my shirt.

"Maybe …" I wasn't going to rule out the possibility, "but not at the hands of this village. Prior to Governor Ryan's stay of the death penalty, lawyers had to take some classes and be granted leave to take on death penalty cases. I never applied. I have no problem handling murder cases but I don't want the responsibility of someone's life."

"So why get involved here?" His voice was squeaking like an adolescent's.

"Now it's too late," I said, thumping the steering wheel for emphasis. "We are *involved*. It is not simply telling a stranger

I won't take the case. If we don't come back, I would feel responsible for her death."

Bob was calming down a bit. Must have been my matching hysteria. "Can you live with yourself if you lose the case and she dies anyway?" he said reasonably.

"I don't know."

"Fine," he said in a flat voice, "let's get the hell out of here." He gestured at the ignition, but I didn't turn the key.

"Do you know why Governor Ryan stayed the death penalty and Governor Quinn abolished the death penalty?"

"No."

He didn't seem particularly interested, but I went on anyway.

"Because the system is flawed. We have the best justice system in the world, but it is still flawed. Too many innocent people have been released due to DNA evidence. Eye witness identification is not reliable. If there is a weapon involved, people tend to look at the gun, not the face of their attacker. Stress can adversely affect memory. People have problems identifying other people of different ethnicities. Confessions are coerced. Hell, people may simply lie."

Bob was still trying to calm me down by speaking slowly and unemotionally. Now he sounded less passionate than if we were discussing a movie. "I'm just saying, if she was killing children and using them for plant fertilizer she deserves to be slow roasted in seven herbs and spices."

"You realize I love her," I said, calmer now.

"You have known her for only a couple of days," he insisted. "I don't know if she put a spell on you or if you were just lonely, but this is not you."

"You don't believe in love at first sight?" I said.

"*You* don't believe in love at first sight," he said. "When it comes to fighting supernatural creatures, you may take ridiculous chances, but not when it comes to love. Maybe you have handled too many divorce cases. When it comes to relationships, you are one of the most cautious people I know. Dude, this is not you."

"Fine," I said, exasperated, "she put a spell on me. It was just like Bette Midler in that movie. Even if it is just a spell and I don't love her, I would still want to help her. This is not about Bridget, it is about getting to the truth."

"The movie is *Hocus Pocus* and that wasn't a love spell. Although the song said something about putting a spell on you. Anyway you are taking me off topic. You are full of it."

I finally turned the key in the ignition and backed out of the driveway at a crazy speed. "Fuck you," I said, "don't you think I would know if someone put a spell on me?"

Seeing Bob hanging on for dear life, I got a grip on myself and slowed down. We drove in silence for a while. The sky was dark, as though it was going to storm, but the air felt cold and dry. The clouds were forming a puffy gray and white quilt in the heavens. The darkness matched my mood.

We passed the Amish household that refused to sell us jam and jelly. In an instant I decided to turn around. I probably should have warned Bob about the U-turn because he looked like he was going to hurl as I spun around at forty-five miles per hour.

"What the hell?" he yelled. "You are going to kill me for just suggesting you got spelled?"

"They know something, I'm sure of it," I said. "Maybe it was what you said about being 'spelled' or maybe it's a hunch. I have to find out."

I pulled into the long driveway and started walking toward the front door. The man we had seen earlier walked out onto the porch. Sure enough, he had his shotgun out and looked prepared to use it.

"You are not welcome here. I told you that before. You can buy your jams and jellies somewhere else. Try hell, for all I care," the man said.

"Put down the gun. I am not the enemy. Those witches did something to you. I just want to talk to you, to help you," I said.

The man did not look convinced. "I can't talk to you. Go away or I'll shoot," he said.

"That's it, isn't it? It is not that you don't want to talk to us, it's that you *can't* talk to us. They have cast a spell of some kind. Show me then. I may be able to help."

The man waved me away with the hand not holding the gun. "It is too late for help. We are way past that."

A woman came out of the house and stood behind him, the girl we'd seen in the barn hanging onto her skirt. The woman tapped him on the shoulder and looked him in the eyes; then she returned to the house. The man allowed the barrel of the gun to point toward the ground. I breathed a sigh of relief.

"I don't trust you two but I will show you," he said, a catch in this throat. "There is nothing you can do for me but maybe it is not too late for others. Follow me."

He led us out behind the house. We passed a clothes line with a few pairs of blue pants and two simple dresses held in place with wooden pins on our way to an old red barn with the door open. I could see six stalls. Only two were occupied by horses; the other four were empty. Behind the barn was a plot of freshly turned earth maybe ten feet long by six feet wide. The man pointed.

It made no sense to dig in the fall when the soil was hard and there was nothing to grow. Why was he showing us this? I could see the sadness in his eyes.

"What is the point of this?" Bob asked the man.

"You asked me to show you."

"Is it a grave?" I asked.

"It is too big for a grave," Bob said.

"Come on," the man said.

"Wait," I said, "the grave isn't for a person. Your cows or horses died. That's why the stalls are empty, isn't it?"

The man turned around to really look at me for the first time. He put the hand without the gun on my shoulder. I could see tears filling his eyes.

"Come on inside," he said.

We returned to the house and he invited us in. The house was smaller than it looked from the outside. The floors were wide-planked pine with simple braided rag rugs spread throughout. The woman sat knitting on an old threadbare couch. The man put the shotgun on a pair of hooks above a large fireplace. The house smelled of burning firewood.

As the man led us up the stairs, they creaked under our weight. He opened the door of the landing to reveal a small room. The room contained a wooden bassinet—no linens or mattress. The bassinet reminded me of an empty human chest with wooden ribs. There was a handmade child's quilt on an oak rack in the corner and a small table with a Bible on it. Otherwise the room was empty. Tears flowed from his eyes and I understood.

"They took your baby, didn't they?" I asked.

In answer he opened the next door on the landing to reveal another small room. There was a small bed and a dresser. The bed was bare. There were no decorations or toys. It was clear no one lived here either.

There was another small room next to the last room he had shown us. The door was ajar. I could see the man's one remaining child resting but still awake on a small daybed. She was sucking her thumb and holding her faceless rag doll close to her chest.

"I have shown you what I can. Now go away," the man said.

"Can I know your name?"

"Yoder, Joseph Yoder. We are not friends. I showed you what I can. I warn you to stay away from that village. Stay away from here as well."

We walked down the stairs and left the house. As we passed I saw Mrs. Yoder's shoulders rise and fall as her chest heaved with sobs, but she made no noise and didn't look up from her knitting. We got back into the car and drove off.

"How did you know?" Bob asked.

"Maybe I'm as psychic as Bridget."

"You believe someone from the village killed those children."

"Yes," I said, "and I'm starting to believe a curse killed their animals as well."

"You think they had a spell put on them just as we had put on us? They can't talk. It is more than just being afraid to talk."

The clouds had thickened in the past half hour and it looked like it was going to storm any minute. I hoped it would hold off until we got off the highway.

"As soon as we get home," I said, "I will put my theory to the test. I am calling the police. I never really believed until now that we were dealing with murder. I thought it was just weird superstition and odd coincidence. If someone was killed, this is a matter for the police, not a coven of witches."

Bob blew out a relieved puff of air. "That is the first thing you have said all day that makes any sense."

CHAPTER THIRTEEN

~~~

WE DROVE IN silence for about ten minutes before I turned on the radio. I must have landed on a station that played old-time radio shows. A deep voice explained how "the weed of crime bares bitter fruit." We were listening to *The Shadow*. I was much too young for *The Shadow*, of course, but my father liked radio shows. I do remember staying up late in my room as a child listening to KMOX out of St. Louis playing *The Mystery Theatre* but I was too young to remember what it was about.

Hearing the old radio show further illustrated how far out of my depth I was. It was not only a matter of ignorance of their customs, but of their history. The coven lived by ancient rules, and I knew nothing of them.

I understood why Bob would think I was under a love spell. I am not inherently impulsive. I am also not in high school. I know what love is—at least to the degree a person can know. I also didn't feel as though I'd been "spelled."

I listened to the radio as we drove north to Champaign. The drainage ditches were filled with yellow flowers and long dead grass. In the mostly empty fields I noticed a large hawk sitting on a mile marker; it noticed me as well, judging from its cold stare.

I pulled off the highway onto Curtis Road, bypassing my neighborhood to take Bob home first. Bob lived in an old section of town near Hassel Park. There were usually not a lot of people walking around there, but as I pulled into his driveway I saw an elderly African American man with a gray beard wearing a T-shirt with the image of a sword stuck into the cotton ground.

"That guy is talking to himself. Do you know him?" I asked Bob.

"No, but he has a Bluetooth in his ear, so he's probably just chatting on the phone."

"Good to know. He looks crazy."

"Well, he could still be talking on the phone to his psychologist at a mental institution or a piece of furniture at home."

"I'll give him the benefit of the doubt," I said. "I'm just jumpy. Although, the image of the sword …. Isn't a sword a symbol of the Tarot?"

"How the hell should I know? You were the one who had your fortune read," Bob said.

We got out of the car and walked into Bob's house. Bob looked concerned. Without speaking, he immediately walked into his kitchen and returned with his Walther PPK in his hand.

"Someone has been here," he whispered. "I never turn off the porch light."

"Maybe you turned it off by accident or maybe the bulb just burned out."

"I will check."

Bob looked at the switch and then went outside. He came back in and returned to the kitchen, carrying a single yellow CFL bulb. He went back out to the porch and returned with the burnt-out bulb.

"All good?"

"Yeah," he said. "This stuff is making me paranoid. Give me a second to pack."

Bob left the room and returned five minutes later with a large duffle bag. He still had a worried scowl on his face, but our situation was so worrisome in general, it could just be that. I figured he'd tell me if what was bothering him was something new.

"I packed you a Beretta."

"Is that what they mean by packing heat?"

"You are hilarious. One of our presidents said, 'Speak softly and carry a big gun.' "

"Big stick," I corrected.

"Same thing," he said.

As we left the house, Bob made a point of showing me that his front porch light was on. I put his bag in the trunk and we drove in the direction of my house. The sky was as gray and depressing as when we left the village, but still no rain. I turned on the radio. A song called "Rude" by the band Magic was playing. I turned off the radio. We drove by Hessel Park and I looked over to where there used to be an old fire truck we played on as kids. The truck was gone, of course. I assume some lawyer or insurance agent forced the park district to remove it. Once again, potential liability trumps actual enjoyment.

Life is about risks. You can't always play it safe. I couldn't let them do this to Bridget. I had to believe she was innocent. We pulled into my driveway and walked into the house.

"This place is nice but it's hard to get used to," Bob said.

"You hang out in here while I pack."

It took me ten minutes to pack two suits, including dress shirts, ties, and shoes. I also packed five T-shirts and five pairs of socks and underwear. I threw in a couple pairs of shorts and sweatpants as well, an iPad mini and a watch. I also pocketed a small fruit knife with a silver blade I kept for luck after a run-in with a demon a few years back.

I returned to the living room, where Bob was watching television. On the travel channel a bald guy with glasses was eating brains. Bob looked up from the screen.

"Are you ready?" I asked.

"Yes, but wasn't there something else we were supposed to do?" he said.

"Get some lunch?"

"Why don't we hit the Amish buffet in Tuscola?" Bob said.

"Sounds good. You are right, though. I feel like we are forgetting something."

He shrugged. "Well, it can't be that important."

As we got into the car I saw a man with long, black and gray hair walking a Labrador. I didn't recognize the man or the dog. He was nicely dressed in khaki pants and a leather jacket. Upon closer inspection he had a tattoo of a pentagram on his neck. He looked to be talking to himself. I did not see a Bluetooth receiver. I was seeing crazy people everywhere.

"Do you get the feeling we're being watched?" I asked Bob.

"Dude, you always say I'm the paranoid one."

"Yeah, I guess you're right."

From my new home it was only a few blocks to the highway. We headed south on I-57 toward Tuscola and stopped at the buffet, where we silently shoveled in large helpings of chicken and dumplings, mashed potatoes, meatloaf, corn, and greens. We were back on the road in less than half an hour.

Bob burped and said, "I was thinking about those Amish people."

"It must have been the buffet."

"If their family was killed, we should call the police."

"Agreed."

It took another forty-five minutes from Tuscola to arrive back at Bridget's. We unloaded the car and walked in the door without knocking. Bridget and Wendy were waiting for us, along with the cat. Alice was not present.

"I will show you to your rooms and then we can prepare a strategy," Bridget said.

My heart sank. "I assumed you and I would be staying together in the room off the library," I said.

KENNEDY

"No," she said gently, "we need to concentrate on the case, not each other. There will be time enough for that after we establish my innocence."

We went through the door leading to the kitchen and up the back stairs to the second level. Bob was given the first room off the stairs. It was a sort of monk's quarters, with a twin bed, nightstand, and dresser. No windows, and the only decoration was an oil painting over the bed of an old castle with the full moon hovering above. Very gothic. Bob put his duffle bag on the bed and followed me to my room next door.

My room had a window, but otherwise the furniture and layout were the same as in Bob's room. My picture was a little less bleak—but only a little. It was a print of Little Red Riding Hood by Gustave Doré. The wolf was bigger than the girl and the illustration was oddly unsettling. I put my suitcase on the bed and followed Bridget and Bob back down the stairs.

We all settled in around the kitchen table.

I spoke first. "I want to finish reading that leather book you gave me, but I can do that later this evening," I said. "Before I do anything else, I want to see those Blood Thorns."

"Wendy will show you," Bridget said.

"Can't you do that or Alice?" Wendy asked, her voice shaking.

"I don't know where Alice is at, and whoever is guarding it is more likely to cooperate with you than me," Bridget said.

"Guarding it?" Wendy said.

"It will be guarded, I do not know by whom. That much power is dangerous if left unattended," Bridget said.

"Fine, follow me," Wendy said, standing. "It's a short walk." Wendy led Bob and me out the back door.

It was three o'clock, but it was fairly dark with the cloud cover. Wendy was clearly uncomfortable as we crossed the country road. We walked through a ditch and into a cornfield. As with the rest of the fields we'd observed, the stalks of corn had been harvested and what remained of the harvest had been cut to about a foot high. As we walked through the field I noticed an island of leafless trees in the distance. In the center of the field was about an acre of untilled wooded area.

I heard the caw of an angry crow in the distance. As we trudged along, Wendy seemed to falter more and more. We had made it about halfway there when she stopped completely.

"Can you guys make it the rest of the way without me?" she said, wiping the sweat from her face, despite the cool breeze. She looked a little green, as if she was going to be sick to her stomach. "You'll find it in the middle of that wooded area. You can't miss it."

"Sure, head on back," I said.

Wendy practically whirled around and headed in the opposite direction at a brisk pace. The closer we got, the more uneasy I felt. I saw a couple of deer in the distance. When we arrived, we were greeted by a large man. I didn't notice him until we stepped between the trees, and his abrupt appearance caused me to gasp.

"Sorry to startle you," he said. "I recognize you as the advocates. I will show you around but you are not to touch anything," the man said.

"Can we ask your name?" I said.

The man had red hair and a beard and was wearing jeans and a beige Carhartt jacket with a black and red flannel shirt underneath. He wore steel-toed Red Wing work boots. He might have been a lumberjack or Yukon Cornelius in *Rudolph the Red-Nosed Reindeer*.

"Calvin," he said. "Follow me."

We walked through the wooded area. The grass was long and hard to get through. It was odd to find no birds or deer in the only place for miles where animals could remain unseen. As we walked, I tripped over something. It was a marble tombstone.

"What the hell?" I said, pointing down at the grave marker.

"Shit, that is creepy," Bob said.

"Everyone in the family who owned this farm before Bridget

is buried here," Calvin explained. "I have found stones that go back to before the civil war. Too bad it is all in such ill repair."

"Bridget's farm?"

"Yes, she is the sole owner of this plot, as well as the hundred acres or so surrounding it. It has been part of her family's estate since the village was founded over a hundred years ago."

Tillable land in this area would sell for between seven thousand and ten thousand dollars per acre. Bridget was sitting on close to a million dollars in land, not including her house. Even the area we were in now had some value. A lot of people in Chicago liked to rent wooded areas for hunting. If her estate went to the coven upon her death, that could be a hell of a good incentive to set her up. I needed to talk with Bridget about that.

The air was cold and smelled clean. As we walked farther along, however, the smell changed to the stink of rotted meat. We must have been two hundred yards or so into the wooded area when we passed a rusted cast-iron fence with spikes along the top. The smell of purification became even more intense. I noticed white marble and gray granite tombstones all around. Most were cracked or broken. I found myself standing upon a small marble stone with the dates 1856–1864; it had a carving of an angel upon it and the words, "My Darling" carved into the pale white surface. A few steps later I saw a carved granite finial that had come from a headstone long since buried under the deep grass.

Calvin stopped and pointed. There was no way I could have prepared for the sight before me. Fifteen feet ahead was a crater, and in the middle was what I could only assume was the object of our search. The plant had a circumference of perhaps six or seven feet. The branches were thick and twisted like the old hemp ropes used by sailors for whaling. Each branch was four inches thick with sharp thorns growing out at random intervals. I noticed a black bird skewered on one of the thorns. The plant's few leaves were gray and small. In the middle was an enormous blood-red trumpet flower. Its shape reminded me of a corpse flower, only slightly larger and far more ominous.

I began to walk down the edge of the crater to get a better look, but Calvin yanked me back. I looked up at him and saw no anger, just concern.

"The Blood Thorns are alive," he said. Taking off his leather backpack, he removed a large plastic bag that contained the body of a dead Canada goose.

He threw the feathered corpse into the middle of the thorns. The branches came alive like an octopus's tentacles and wrapped around the large bird; then they were still once again. As I looked more carefully I noticed bones—human bones?— around the outside of the plant.

"Do you always carry a dead goose with you?" I asked.

"No, the elders knew you were going to come and asked me to provide a demonstration," he said.

"I hope that wasn't your dinner," I said.

"Not anymore," Calvin replied.

"Are these the bones of the victims you claim Bridget is responsible for?" I asked.

"Yes," Calvin said.

"We are in a cemetery," I said. "How do you know the bones are not from the graves? Were they carbon dated or tested for DNA to determine the identity of the deceased?"

"I don't know. Ask Mr. Levi. If you look farther, though, it's pretty clear." Calvin pointed to a piece of cloth that was once a shirt in the mass of branches. It was covered in what I assumed was human blood.

"Did they gather some of this clothing to test it for blood?" I asked.

He shuddered. "No one has entered. Most people value their lives more than that. I was the only member of the coven who would agree to do a demonstration."

I took some pictures using my iPhone and then Bob and I left. Calvin remained at the edge of the wooded area. I was chilled to the bone, despite the temperature being perfectly pleasant. As Bob and I headed back to Bridget's, I could feel dread in the air.

We walked through the door to find Wendy and Bridget in front of the fireplace. It looked as though we had interrupted an intense conversation. Neither woman stood or reacted to our presence. It was not until Bob and I pulled up a chair that anyone spoke.

"What do you think?" Bridget asked.

"It was horrible," Bob said.

"It is what happens when nature is defiled," Bridget said. "Magic can be used to alter and transform nature. I have seen fluffy bunnies who crave human flesh and apples filled with blood. Blood Thorns are an abomination, but I did not create this plant."

"Is that where we get blood oranges?" Bob said.

"You are hilarious," Wendy said, narrowing her eyes at him.

"How are they going to tie you to this?" I said. "What evidence do they have? Also, can they prove that children were taken in the first place and if so, how could they possibly prove you are behind it?"

"I don't know what evidence they have or plan to use," Bridget said.

"Also, if you are killed, what happens to your estate? That could be a motive to set you up, assuming your estate would go to the coven. I guess I don't know if you have any children."

"I don't have any children. If I die the estate goes back to the coven. My great-great aunt essentially gave me and my family the use of the lands, but if there is no natural heir, the family line dies out and the land reverts to the coven."

"I need a copy of the will."

"A copy is included in the book I gave you. You haven't finished it, then."

"No."

"Why don't you do that while we get dinner? It will give you an idea of the procedure for the hearing. We can make plans while we eat. "

Chapter Fourteen

~~~

The book was still on the table where I'd left it. Bob, Wendy, and Bridget headed to the kitchen. I skipped through the pages until I found the heading, PROCEDURE FOR A HEARING FOR A VIOLATION OF THE COVEN'S RULES:

> Whomever is charged with a violation of any of the central tenets of magic will be entitled to a public hearing. A member of each family representing the original five elders will be in attendance and will participate, provided he or she is of an age and proper mental state to do so. One elder will present the case against the accused. The remaining members will act as judges. If a member of the elders is accused then the remaining elders will judge the accused. Guilt must be decided by a unanimous vote. A minimum of three people will act as judges. Should the family line of the original elders die out, leaving fewer than three judges, then the remaining judges will select additional judges from the coven to ensure that at least three people will be on the panel. There can be no punishment for guilt other than death by fire for those in violation of the central tenets.

> All evidence may be considered but the weight said

evidence is given is at the discretion of the judges. No finding of death can be based solely on the actions of the accused's ancestors. No finding of death can be based solely on a statement made by a person who does not stand before the tribunal. No finding of death may be based solely on spells for the purpose of obtaining truth. Any spells to obtain the truth must be performed before the entire coven.

Other than the accused, all witnesses must submit to a truth spell before making a statement before the hearing. The accused need not testify. Should he or she choose to testify, the accused need not submit to a truth spell. Testimony without a truth spell will not carry the same weight as testimony after a truth spell is administered.

The testimony of a witness as to statements made outside of the public hearing that was obtained by use of magic and/or torture will be given little weight. Statements of animals, inanimate objects, demons, or creatures from the netherworld are admissible but will be given less weight than those of a coven member or a non-magical creature.

The accused has the following rights. The accused may choose his or her own advocate(s). Advocate(s) will be given full cooperation in their investigation. The accused may choose to testify. The accused may complete the death ceremony prior to the burning.

The coven has the following rights upon a finding of guilt. The coven may search the home of the guilty for books and tools used for black magic. The coven may permanently expel from the coven any family members of the guilty party from the community. If the witch has a familiar, it will be destroyed at the discretion of the coven.

I put down the book. This was not going to be easy. It looked as though this crazy tribunal could do whatever the

hell they liked. I could smell fresh baked rolls and walked into
the kitchen. Bob and Wendy seemed in the middle of a deep
conversation. Bridget was taking a loaf of pumpkin bread out
of the oven. She had a black caldron on the stove, a smaller
version of the cast-iron ones used by witches on Halloween
greeting cards. From the smell I was guessing it contained a
hearty beef stew.

"Go ahead and put these dishes on the table," Bridget said.
"We have the rest of the evening and tomorrow before the
hearing begins. I want to get started."

I tried to wrap my arms around her in a supportive hug, but
she pushed me aside. I was unsure if she was uncomfortable
with the public display of affection or just uncomfortable
with me. Given that she could be put to death in a few days, I
attributed her brush-off to the circumstances.

We all had a seat at the table and Wendy lit two large
beeswax candles. Bridget sat down at the table and covered
her eyes as she said a blessing to thank the earth, rain, and
sun for our meal. The cauldron did contain a beef stew. There
was also sliced pumpkin that was more savory than sweet, she
explained, and green beans.

"I have apple pie, pumpkin bread, and bread pudding for
dessert," Bridget said.

"Excellent," Bob said, licking his lips.

We filled our plates with food and began to eat. Bob was
enjoying his meal more than I was. Bridget's mind was clearly
elsewhere. She had hardly touched her stew. We sat eating in
silence for around ten minutes when the calm gave way to the
sound of an old school bell ringing over and over again.

"We have to get to the meeting place," Wendy said, panic in
her voice. "Something has happened."

"What is it?" I asked.

Bridget was already on her feet. "Let's go," she said urgently.
"There's no time to waste."

By the time we had got to the meeting place the rest of the

coven was already there. Mr. Levi was standing on the porch waiting for us to arrive. Even from where we stood, twenty or so feet away, he looked upset.

"Our sister Alice is dead," Mr. Levi announced.

It did not seem possible. Alice had been with us this morning. When she left I figured she just got hung up in the store.

"How?" someone in the crowd called out.

"Murdered, and we will find out who is responsible," Mr. Levi said.

"What of the outsiders? The advocates? Where were they when this happened?" a woman with long blonde hair and wearing a black wool coat demanded.

"What of the accused?" a bearded man yelled. "It must have something to do with her."

"She was my friend!" Bridget cried out. "I loved Alice. She was one of the few of this coven willing to stand with me. I would have no reason to kill her nor would my advocates. The true dark witch or warlock did it in an effort to undermine my defense. The witch is trying to destroy my supporters. To scare off those who believe in me. To see me burn so she or he can continue to thrive."

"We will not resolve this by yelling," Mr. Levi said. "Go back to your homes. We will investigate. Please keep your doors and windows locked. None of us is safe."

The crowd began to disperse, but the four of us remained. I walked up to Mr. Levi. Bridget tried to grab me but I nudged her aside. Clearly Bridget was annoyed at my boldness for approaching the man on my own.

"I want to see the body and the murder scene," I said.

"Why?"

"Because it seems an odd coincidence for a murder to take place immediately prior to the trial. It is odder still that the victim would be one of the two witches who are standing by the accused."

"You are not a part of our coven."

"The procedural rules of the coven require full cooperation with the advocate. Do you wish to deny Ms. Gillis this right?" I said.

"You may come, alone, right now. You may not touch anything. You may not talk to anyone outside of the coven."

"All right," I said.

"Bridget, Wendy, and the other advocate …" Mr. Levi paused.

"Bob," Bob said.

"Yes, Bob … of course. I am taking Mr. Roberts to see … Alice. The rest of you go back home."

"She is my friend," Bridget said. "I want to go."

"You may make an appeal to the other elders. For now, the answer is no." Mr. Levi turned to walk away. I followed, preparing myself mentally for what lay ahead.

We walked in silence until we arrived in front of the three stores we had visited earlier. Had Alice been murdered in her own store? The plate glass window was covered with sheets of brown paper. I assumed it was the same type of paper she wrapped meat and food items in.

"She is in here," Mr. Levi said. "I hope you have a strong stomach."

Chapter Fifteen

~~~

W<small>E WALKED UP</small> to the entrance of the store. I could hear movement within. Mr. Levi knocked on the door and Abraham Mage opened it. I recognized Mr. Mage from the meeting. He looked older than when I had seen him just hours ago.

"Who is with you?" Mr. Mage asked.

"Sam Roberts, one of the advocates," Mr. Levi responded.

"Why?"

"In the event the cases are related, he feels he has the right to be here. I agree."

"I hope he has a strong stomach."

The door opened and I braced myself for the smell of death. Instead I was greeted with the scent of bleach and lavender. If anything, the store was cleaner than when I'd last been here. The shelves were undisturbed. There were no broken doors or windows.

"She is in the case," Mr. Mage said, pointing to the refrigerated glass case that had been stocked with meats and cheeses on our last visit.

The bottom of the case held thick blocks of ice. To my horror it was filled with what remained of Alice. In a neat row lay her organs. I recognized the liver, kidneys, heart, and bladder.

The next row had intestines curled up like a snake as well as the stomach and a heap of viscera I could not identify. Next to the organs was Alice's head. Her mouth and eyelids were closed, and upon closer inspection I noted what I thought was a piece of thread coming down from her left eye. I wondered if the lids had been sewn shut. The stump resting in the ice kept the head propped up and facing the room. One of her thighs from the hip to her knee was next, followed by both her arms cut at the elbow and ending at the wrist. Both severed hands were together, the fingers forming a steeple as though in prayer. Under the tiny tent made by her hands were her tongue, eyeballs, and ten or so teeth. This was followed by both her feet. The nails were painted a bright red.

It took me a while to adjust to what I was seeing. There was a bulletin board behind the case that I assumed must normally contain a list of daily specials. On the board was written: "eye for eye, tooth for tooth, hand for hand, foot for foot—Exodus 21:24." More disturbing yet, I noted that next to each cut of meat in the case was a chrome price holder. Each held a handwritten paper card describing the cut and price in neat script:

Witch's liver—$1 per pound
The head of a Witch—$17
The heart of a Witch—$5

The entire case was filled with these cards, describing body parts and prices.

On a low counter that pushed up to the back side of the case next to the sliding doors was an old-fashioned hog scraper, a few knives, and a bone saw. The tools looked antique. Yet, despite their age, the metal surfaces were clean and rust-free.

"Where is the rest of the body?" I asked. "There are no ribs or skin, and we are missing other parts as well."

"This is all we found," Mr. Levi said.

"There should be blood as well. This ice is mostly clear. The blood must have been drained," I said.

"I am sure the witch collected the blood for dark magic," Mr. Mage said.

"First of all," I said, "why would a witch provide a biblical reference? Also, Alice was at the meeting at around noon. It is a little after eight now. That does not give a person a lot of time to butcher a witch and drain her blood. Not to mention the individual price tags. Whoever did this was a surgeon or butcher. If I had to guess, given the time involved, we are looking for more than one person."

"I have no idea. I need time to think," Mr. Levi said.

"It is outside of any of our areas of expertise," I said. "We need to call the police. They can look for fingerprints, maybe analyze the writing on the board and cards, and search for the remainder of the body."

Mr. Levi scowled. "This is the business of the coven. You may not call the police. We have cast a spell and you have agreed."

"This has nothing to do with Bridget's case," I said.

"Earlier you said it did."

"I changed my mind after seeing the evidence."

"Do what you want," Mr. Levi said. "You can argue whatever you like before the tribunal. I think we are done here. Abraham, lock up. I will walk Mr. Roberts out."

Reluctantly I left with Mr. Levi and we walked in silence toward the fortune teller's home. When we approached an olive green Victorian house, Mr. Levi started to veer toward it.

"I want to talk to you about the evidence you intend to present at the hearing," I called after him. "I need to know what the witnesses have to say and how to locate them."

He turned his head but did not stop. "Come by tomorrow at nine. I am done for the night."

His skin was a ghastly shade of gray, and under normal circumstances I'd have let him go.

"Mr. Levi," I said firmly, "I must insist. The trial is the day after tomorrow. That gives me very little time."

"I knew Alice," he said flatly. "I know her family. I have plans for the rest of the evening. I will see you in the morning."

I kept thinking about the body. Bridget would not have killed her good friend. She wouldn't have had time to lay out such a ghastly display. I'd been with her a good portion of the day. I was going to return to her house, and when I got there, I would call the police.

CHAPTER SIXTEEN

～～

W HEN I GOT back to Bridget's, everyone was in the front room, waiting to hear about Alice. When I shared what I had observed, they looked sick.

"What does it all mean?" Wendy asked.

"Whoever did this, did so because Alice was an ally," Bridget said.

"I don't think it was a witch," I said, "since they quoted the Bible. Who in the coven is a surgeon or butcher?"

"Alice was something of a butcher—I mean, she would cut and trim meat for her store—but no one else," Wendy said.

"What about a hunter?" Bob asked. "If a hunter can field dress a buck then couldn't he do this?"

I stopped my pacing and said, "Maybe, but this goes way beyond a field dressing. To remove the organs without damaging them takes skill. Also, the display required a bit of flair."

"Why don't we have a look around tonight?" Bob said. "If we can find the blood, skin, and bones it might lead us to the killer."

I caught a glimpse of Bridget out of the corner of my eye. I could see a measure of hope in her eyes.

"I agree," I said, "but it may not be possible. Given all the hunters this time of year, someone could throw the remains into a dumpster without attracting attention. I also have a feeling whoever did this is cautious and wouldn't make it easy."

"If you could get some of her blood and bones, I could raise her spirit," Bridget said. "Then we could ask her."

"Are you insane?" Wendy said, her voice rising. "Number one, someone will be guarding the body. Number two, those spells are forbidden. How could you even consider it?"

"Sorry," Bridget said. "Of course we can't. I'm just desperate."

I shook my head. "I can't think of much we can do tonight. Without knowing who the witnesses are, I have no idea who to interview. I would like to go over the physical evidence as well, but again, I'm in the dark. In the morning Bob and I will talk to Mr. Levi and find out what he is willing to share. Once we do that then we can start our investigation."

Wendy raised her hand. "I'll help."

"I better run things from here," Bridget said, "and let you guys do the interviews. I suspect no one will be comfortable talking with me."

"If you don't mind," I said, "I'd like to go through your library tonight. Look up what I can about 'Blood Thorns' and 'witches' tribunals.' Maybe you can help me find what I'm looking for." I looked directly at Bridget.

"I will help you find a couple of books," she said, "but the loss of Alice is too much for me. We were sisters. Please let me grieve alone for the remainder of the evening."

I followed Bridget to the third floor. She selected two books; one had a leather binding. The front and back boards were not leather but instead had ornate marbling. The second volume was older and the cover was separate from the binding. She handed them to me without making eye contact.

"These belonged to my great-great aunt. They do contain references to dark magic. I have not read through them completely. I have thousands of books on magic and these are hard to read. The language is a bit archaic."

"I understand you need to be alone," I said gently, "but if we're not prepared for this trial, you will be joining Alice."

I wanted to touch her but managed to keep my hands to myself.

"Are you always this insensitive?"

I sighed. "There is nothing anyone can do for Alice. It isn't too late for you. We have one full day to get ready. We can't be distracted. For all we know, the true evil doer did this to Alice in order to distract you."

"I have given you what you asked for," she said, hugging herself. "Please go away." She turned and wandered off.

I went to my room. I was pissed at Bridget but had to remind myself that her friend was dead and she might be next. Grief and impending doom could have a negative impact on anyone's disposition.

When I got there Bob was sitting in the position we used to call Indian style but now is probably referred to as Native American style or crisscross applesauce to the more politically correct. His back was to a wall and his laptop was open. He looked up to acknowledge my entrance and then looked back down at the computer.

"I have been researching this community on the Internet," Bob said. "By the way, I am wasting a lot of my data plan. Are witches too good for Wi-Fi?"

"Well, witches melt in water," I replied. "Maybe the idea of surfing the Web is too scary."

"I don't get it," he said.

"You surf in water and the wicked witch in *The Wizard of Oz* melted because of a bucket of water."

"Hilarious," Bob said. "Did you see the musical, *Wicked*?"

"No, but I read the book."

"How can you make a musical a book?"

"The musical wasn't made into a book. They based the musical on a book."

"How was it?" he said.

"A bit depressing but good," I said. "The book is by Gregory Maguire. The Wicked Witch of the West was picked on as a child and Glinda, The Good Witch, was shallow and vapid. Although I'm more interested in what you found during your search."

He frowned. "Oddly, virtually nothing. The village stores share a single Web page to sell items. Mr. Levi has written a couple articles on ancient texts. He has a decent reputation as a scholar and graduated from Oxford University. I have no idea how he wound up in Illinois."

"Anyone have financial problems? Some reason to kill Bridget for her money?"

"You don't need financial problems to want money."

"What about missing children?" I said. "If kids were being taken there would have to be newspaper reports."

"None in this area within the past couple of years ... other than college kids related to our favorite fraternity."

"That's odd," I said. "Keep looking. I'm going to skim these books Bridget gave me."

"All right," he said, closing his laptop. "I'm going back to my room. Come running if you hear me scream. This place has got to be loaded with ghosts."

"You're just assuming it's haunted because a witch lives here?" I said.

"Which witch? Wendy is spending the night," Bob said.

"You just wanted to say 'which witch,' " I said. "Where is Wendy at?"

"You shouldn't end a sentence with a preposition."

"Where is Wendy at ... asshole?"

"Isn't that the punchline of a joke involving a Texan and a guy from Harvard?"

"Just answer the question."

"I don't know," he said with a shrug. "Third floor, I think."

"I'd like to get her opinion on who might want to kill Alice."

"Maybe you should wait for the morning," he said. "She seemed a bit freaked out."

"I guess. All right, I am going to skim through these books and then get some sleep. We have a big day tomorrow."

"Do you want the Beretta to put under your pillow?"

"No, I'm fine."

"Now that I think about it, didn't Casper the Friendly Ghost hang out with a witch named Wendy?"

"That does support your ghost in the house theory, but there is only one problem."

"What?"

"We are not in a fucking comic book."

With some difficulty Bob got up, retrieved the computer and cord, and left my room. I wasn't worried about ghosts, but I was worried. I didn't trust this system of justice.

I picked up the first book and checked the table of contents. The chapter on Blood Thorns sounded like a good place to start. It appeared that the seed for the Blood Thorns had to be removed from the "infernal regions of the place of torment" then germinated in the blood of an innocent until the blood spoiled.

The plant fed on blood and was able to move and feed on its own after six months. The witch could control its movements, but the plant couldn't be moved from where it was planted. The Blood Thorns produced a single fruit. If eaten, it enhanced the powers of the person who consumed it.

I wanted to know specifically what additional power it provided to the witch. I assumed the information would be on the next page, but it wasn't. Oddly, upon closer inspection, I realized that the next page had been removed. There was no jagged edge to the paper, which had been cut very close to the binding. The surgery on the book would take a bit of skill, but my guess was a book dealer like Mr. Levi would have more than enough skill for the task.

I skipped ahead to a chapter about communication with the dead. I had to admit I was curious if we could bring Alice back. Discovering her murderer might resolve everything. The book did not include spells but it did include basic information about what needed to be done and how it worked.

Raising the dead physically as well as spiritually required the spilling of blood. To open a hole in the world that separated the living and dead, blood was always required. To revive the physical form of the deceased required buckets. For just the spirit, not as much. Although it was not unknown for a spirit to return in animal form, the apparition normally appeared as it had near the time the person had died—only partially transparent, as if formed from smoke. To raise the physical form meant bidding the corpse to dig its way out of the grave. It could bring back a rotting, fetid mess. It was also not possible if the body had been cremated or buried too long ago.

The danger in casting such spells was not knowing what would return. Opening even the tiniest hole between the world of the living and the world of the dead could revive unwanted spirits. Demons could disguise themselves as ghosts or the spirts of the recently deceased.

Evil wizards, witches, and warlocks had been known to control the spirits of the dead and use them to do their bidding. These spells could disrupt the balance between the world of the living and dead.

I skipped ahead to the chapter on Blood Curses. The curses included some of the plagues cast upon the pharaoh in the book of Exodus as well as others unpleasantness. I read through the list: water to blood, lice, cattle sickness, crop disease, madness, muteness, boils, blindness, and death. Casting any of these spells required the blood of an innocent. I understood why these spells were all forbidden by the coven.

Exhausted, I decided to get some sleep, although I suspected that after my light reading, sleep would be hard to come by. I put the books down on the dresser and closed my eyes.

CHAPTER SEVENTEEN

～～～

I OPENED MY eyes to find myself in front of a small supermarket, which reminded me from the outside of the stores in the village. As I walked in I heard a man singing "Lost in a Supermarket" by The Clash. The store was bigger than Alice's, at least twice the size.

In the middle of the store was the singer—a man taking a shower while standing in an old, white, claw-foot bathtub. A curved free-standing shower nozzle rained water down on him. The tub was surrounded by a shower curtain that was clear, except for some opaque goldfish that seemed to swim through the air. He was using a wooden shower brush as a microphone. He turned off the water and looked at me.

"I am the great and powerful Wizard of Oz. Do not look behind the curtain," the man said.

"Are you kidding me?" I asked.

"Of course I am kidding."

The man put down his brush and stared at me. He was probably in his late sixties, with long, puffy gray hair parted in the middle. I felt I should know him, but given that he was naked and I was seeing him through a shower curtain it was hard to be certain.

"You look familiar," I said.

"I should," he replied. "I am the Reverend Cotton Mather from the Salem Witch Trials."

"You don't sound like a reverend from the sixteen hundreds."

"It's your dream. Besides, I died in 1728 but I didn't stop living. I have changed with the times."

"That Clash tune is from 1979; you haven't exactly kept up."

"I tell you what," he said. "Why don't you look around and do your shopping? I will also give you some advice, unless you think you know everything."

"I'm listening."

"Never raise the dead."

"Thank you."

"While I'm at it, I'll give you some more advice."

"Okay."

"Turn off your cellphone in movie theaters. Don't pee on an electric fence. Finally, don't whistle if you don't mean it and don't growl if you can't bite."

He turned the shower back on and returned to singing. The song was the same but the water was different. It had turned the color of blood.

I began looking through the store. There was a long shelf stocked with strange cereals. First, I picked up a box of 'Fruit Hoops,' with a picture of a crow spinning a basketball on his beak on the front of the box. More disturbing was the 'Hew Berry'; the box bore an image of a man with an axe cutting up a woman and stacking her body parts like cordwood. The 'Frosted Snakes' box showed a boy digging into a bowl overflowing with serpents, and 'Death' cereal depicted the Grim Reaper cutting down stalks in a field of oats.

If the cereals were not disturbing enough by themselves, the rats and mice sharing the shelves and chewing on the cardboard certainly compounded the horror. All of a sudden the outrageous amounts of sugar and corn syrup in my normal breakfast choices seemed like healthy alternatives. I knew it was a mistake but I walked over to the glass case that should have housed the deli meats.

The case appeared the same as the one that had served as Alice's repository in my waking hours, with the organs arranged neatly in a row, followed by other cuts of human meat. When I got to Alice's head, the eyelids opened, revealing empty sockets. I assumed it was an illusion until the head began to speak.

"Can I help you?" Alice's head said.

"No offense," I said, "but you are the one in need of help. You have been parceled out and put on display."

"My liver is quite tender," the head said. "I rarely drank. I would stay away from my colon. I have not been eating well because of the whole situation with Bridget. My bowels have been a bit irritable. Witches tend to have a higher rate of Crohn's Disease and Irritable Bowel Syndrome than that of the regular population."

"May I ask you a question?"

"Ask me whatever you like. Although I suspect the answer is to cook it under a low heat with olive oil, garlic, and onions."

"Who murdered you?"

"I don't know, but perhaps a better question is who didn't murder me. I would have preferred they use an athame or at least a power saw."

"Who didn't murder you?"

"I did not recognize them. Doesn't that tell you something?"

"They?"

"There were two of them. Can't talk anymore. There is another customer and I want to concentrate on looking delicious."

I turned around to see a semi-transparent dark figure in a black robe. The sight of him sent a chill through me. I walked over to what I assumed was the produce section of the store.

There were red apples lined up in neat rows. A sign read, "Stepmother Brand Wishing Apples—fifty cents each." Next to the apples were pint-sized baskets of black berries labeled "Belladonna fruit," followed by rows of roots that resembled tiny people labeled "mandrake root." As I stood looking at the produce, the misters turned on, spraying me with water, and an instrumental version of "It's Raining Men" by the Weather Girls played through invisible speakers. I felt a tap on my shoulder and turned around.

Behind me stood a living skeleton. He was wearing a white bib apron and a white shirt with a bow tie. His white hat reminded me of the type the staff wore at Steak and Shake. This was how I imagined grocers from the 1950s looked—other than the whole living skeleton part.

"I thought you came for the fruit of the Blood Thorns," the skeleton said.

"How can you talk without a larynx?" I asked.

"I don't know," the skeleton replied. "How could Alice's head talk without a tongue? Maybe we both are dreaming. The point is we only have one if you want to see it."

"One what?"

"One fruit from the Blood Thorns."

"Oh, of course. Is it ripe?"

"Not until All Hallow's Eve. You must have a look. They are rarely in stock. Please follow me."

He led me through a swinging double door behind the counter to a refrigerated room with a large metal table at its center. In the middle of the table was a woven basket filled with straw. Next to it was a wood cutting board with the words, "Boo Block" and the image of a ghost burned into the wood. There was a long knife next to it.

"You wait here, and I will get it. It is awfully cold for me. Please forgive the rattling of my bones. That was the one part of being alive I miss, the old bone dance. Now I just rattle."

He left and came back with a shoebox in his hands. On the side were the words "Blood Thorn Fruit—handle with care" written in black magic marker. He placed the box next to the board and opened the lid slowly. He removed the yellowish red fruit and placed it in the basket as carefully as if it were an egg.

"You can see it is almost ripe," the skeleton said. "If you pick it up and smell the end where the stem was, you can tell. You can also thump it. It should produce a whimper."

The fruit was heavy for its size, maybe four pounds. At first it looked oblong like a Korean melon. Upon closer inspection it had the outline of a baby in the fetal position. I smelled the stem, which reeked of rotten meat, and thumped it, which made it shake as though alive. I quickly put it down, alarmed by my discovery.

"I don't want it," I said.

"Well, it's not ripe yet," the skeleton said. "I wish I could eat some. It would put flesh back on these old bones. They sometimes make noise."

I picked up the melon and held it to my ear. It began to shake on its own again. Then I did hear a noise—like a whimpering kitten.

I opened my eyes to see Bridget's black cat. It was meowing at me. I picked up my iPhone. It was eight a.m. and we had to meet Mr. Levi soon. I threw on a T-shirt and sweatpants and walked downstairs. Everyone else was sitting around the table eating breakfast.

"Damn," Bob said, "it's not like you to sleep late. Bridget sent her cat up to wake you."

"Smart cat," I said.

"Sit down and eat," Bridget said. "There is coffee, tea, and orange juice on the side table." She placed a plate in front of me with a buttermilk biscuit, a blueberry muffin, and two fried eggs on it.

"Is everyone coming to speak with Mr. Levi?" I asked.

"No, just you and Bob, my advocates. Come back when you're done. I suspect we'll have a lot to do. The hearing starts first thing in the morning and I do not particularly look forward to the prospect of being cooked like this biscuit." She held up the biscuit by way of example.

"More like a roasted pig," Bob amended. "Not that you are

pig-like … I mean the fire part of it … not that I think that is going to happen."

"Bob and I should get going," I said, "as soon as he takes his foot out of his mouth."

Bridget's beautiful lips were pursed in disapproval. "That is an excellent idea," she said.

I got up and walked out the front door, but not before I was confronted by the cat, who was definitely giving me a dirty look. Bob didn't seem to want to leave the table, but in a minute he followed after me.

CHAPTER EiGHTEEN

~~~

"WHAT'S YOUR HURRY?" Bob said. "I haven't taken a shower yet."

"Neither have I," I said, "but we can't risk being late. Plus, if I left you in there any longer you'd have gotten yourself turned into a toad."

"Can she do that?"

"I'm not sure, but do you want to find out?"

Bob looked a little sheepish. "You know that voice in your head that tells you to shut up?" he asked.

"Yes."

"Mine may be defective."

I snorted. "No shit, Sherlock. You should be a member of the FBI."

"Hey, that's my line," Bob said, punching me in the shoulder.

"I have an idea," I said, holding up an index finger. "When we meet with Mr. Levi, let me do the talking."

We arrived at Mr. Levi's olive green Victorian house, two houses down from Bridget's. I hadn't noticed before, but the architecture of Mr. Levi's Victorian was identical to Bridget's, other than the color. I remembered that Bridget had said the original five homes were all built by her great-great aunt. It was probably cheaper and easier to construct the same house over and over again.

We walked up the porch stairs and knocked on the door. Mr. Levi opened it a few minutes later. He was wearing black pants, a green button-down shirt, and a tweed jacket. He looked professorial, as usual, and very tense, also as usual. It was clear we were underdressed.

"Come in," Mr. Levi said. His voice couldn't have been less inviting.

He pointed us to a large sofa before an unlit fireplace. The layout of the house was similar to Bridget's but that was where their similarities ended. Mr. Levi had massive antique furniture that looked like it had been made by the same manufacturer and had always been a set. Most of it was mahogany. The windows had thick velvet drapes blocking the sun. Mr. Levi's house lacked the picture windows featured in Bridget's solarium. Instead he'd used the space to house bookshelves filled with ancient volumes. The house was dark and imposing. Bob and I shared the rather uncomfortable couch and Mr. Levi sat across from us.

"Why are you here?" Mr. Levi asked. He leaned forward in his chair and gazed at us with stern intensity.

"Didn't you invite us to go over the evidence?" I countered.

"That isn't what I meant. Why are you involved?"

"I don't know," I said. "I guess I'm strange in that I don't like the idea of barbecuing people. Particularly innocent ones."

"We will see," he said. "I have found a book. It is dated to the mid-nineteenth century and belonged to a witch named Hazel Waterhouse. It contains a detailed description of how she helped the great-great aunt of Bridget Gillis, Bridget Bishop, grow Blood Thorns. I have made a photocopy of the pages."

"Who cares what a relative did over a hundred years ago?" I said.

"It shows that a member of her family was aware of how to perform this very complicated spell. A member of her family she was named after. The instructions were likely passed down from her."

"Hell, *you* have the book," I said, waving my hands at him. "So *you* definitely have the instructions. *You* certainly know how to grow Blood Thorns. You are only speculating that she has instructions or knows how to grow Blood Thorns."

"Make your arguments tomorrow."

"I want to see the rest of the book. Put it in context."

"The book is very valuable. It is not leaving my house."

"Then I will examine it while I'm here."

"Fine."

"What other evidence do you have?"

"I have spoken with a man named Tim Johnson. He is not a member of the coven or Amish but he has a small house not far from here. He saw Bridget running through the field near the Blood Thorns with a baby. Actually it may have been a young child."

"Do you have an address and telephone number?" I asked.

"I have made a list of everyone I was able to find contact information for. I will give it to you before you go." Mr. Levi paused, then continued, "I have spoken to an Amish family who will testify they had two of their three children taken from them and were put under a spell that forbids them from speaking of it."

"How can they testify if they've been spelled?" Bob asked.

"We will help them," Mr. Levi said.

"What other evidence do you have?" I asked.

"I will call Serena Parker; she is a sister of the coven. She will testify that last year before Samhain, Bridget left a pie pan of blood by her door to feed evil spirits."

"Did she taste it to find out if it was blood?" I asked. "There are many Halloween traditions involving food and drink. Including leaving wine out."

"There is Souling and Guising," Bob added.

Mr. Levi looked supremely annoyed. "What are you talking about?" he asked, wrinkling his nose.

"Souling is a tradition from the British Isles of providing food and drink on Halloween in exchange for people coming to your door and praying for dead relatives," Bob explained. "Guising is a tradition where people provide food and drink in exchange for singing or dancing. Another Halloween tradition. My point is that Halloween is traditionally a time to put out food or in this case drink. Leaving wine out would not be unheard of."

Mr. Levi looked stunned by Bob's knowledge of such arcane traditions. I wasn't surprised. Bob has an endless supply of seemingly worthless information stockpiled on a large variety of subjects.

"You can make whatever points you want to make at the tribunal," Mr. Levi said.

"Anything else?" I asked.

"Bethany Montgomery will testify that she has heard noises coming from the house at all hours of the night, including the sounds of children."

"Do you have people who will testify that Bridget built a gingerbread hut out back to draw the children in?" I asked.

"To think you yelled at me for saying what I was thinking earlier today," Bob said, giving me a wounded look.

Mr. Levi cleared his throat ostentatiously. "Mr. Roberts, we are not prosecuting Ms. Gillis for being a witch. We are all witches and warlocks. This is not Salem or a fairytale. We are not going to have a Monty Python style duck weighing or a recreation of the Salem Witch Trials. I find discrimination against our kind abhorrent. That is why we are doing this. We have lived among our neighbors here for over a century and have created a utopia. If the outside word finds out that one of us is killing their children it will all start again. We will all be burned, not just one of us. One life for the sake of the entire village is a fair trade. So get off your high horse and do your job. I personally hope I am wrong. I would love it if you are successful."

"The soul of every member of this village will be diminished if a single innocent person is killed," I said.

"I don't know if Bridget told you this," he said, "but I love her. We were engaged to be married once."

"That is why you want her dead? Punishment for leaving you?"

"You do not understand; I still love her. If I believed even for a moment she was innocent I would do anything possible to end this. Yet, beyond any doubt, I know that she is not." As Mr. Levi spoke I could see a tear escaping his right eye. He brushed it away.

"You don't see a conflict with her former lover being her prosecutor?"

"I don't expect you to understand."

"Fine, what other evidence do you intend to present?" I said.

"I will show the coven the Blood Thorns and the growing fruit. All were cultivated on her land."

"What else?"

"Isn't that enough?"

"No," I said, gritting my teeth.

"We will see." He handed me a piece of paper. "Here is the list of witnesses with their names and addresses. I would skip the Amish couple; they will not be able to speak with you. Tim Johnson may not speak with you but you can try. The coven members have an obligation to cooperate."

I handed the list to Bob. "Bob, would you take the list and the photocopies of the passage from the book Mr. Levi referenced back to Bridget? I want to stick around and skim through the original volume."

Bob got up and left. Mr. Levi led me to a small room, similar in size and shape to the one where Bridget read my fortune … or hers, as it turned out. In Mr. Levi's home this room was a small library. He pointed to an ornately carved walnut desk with a leather pad. There were a number of oak lawyer's bookshelves against two of the walls. Behind the glass doors were many more ancient volumes. A single book lay on the desk, leather bound and unmarked. A feather was used to bookmark a page.

There was a smaller desk against one of the walls with a laptop computer and an all-in-one printer. It seemed out of place in a house filled with antiques. Perhaps that is why this place was so unsettling. It was the juxtaposition of the modern with the archaic.

He made a broad gesture toward the book. "The volume is marked to the proper page. Feel free to skim through the rest of it. Please wear the white cotton gloves next to the book. If you need to copy any pages, ask me. Do you understand?" Mr. Levi was pacing the room with his usual stiff strides as he recited his demands.

"Yes," I said, picking up the gloves and putting them on to show good faith.

"Good, I'll be around. If you don't need anything else, you may let yourself out when you are done. Is there anything else?"

"Yes," I said, "may I ask why you and Bridget broke up?"

"No," Mr. Levi said and left the room.

CHAPTER NiNETEEN

~~~

T HE BOOK'S COVER had once had a title or some other markings and the writing had faded over time. Between two raised bands on the spine was a large H.W. painted in gold leaf that had mostly faded away. It was clear this book was well used and important to the owner.

The endpapers had a marbled pattern of swirled purple. This book would have been very expensive in its day. The inside endpaper cover had the name *Hazel Waterhouse*, written in ornate script. The H and the W were formed of twirled green branches painted by hand. Below the name was a large Roman numeral I and below that, a handwritten scrawl, "*With love that will defy time and extend into the beyond—Bridget.*"

The handwritten script made it tough going, not to mention that the prose was written in an antiquated style of English by someone who was clearly from the British Isles. It was interesting, but I was in a hurry and had to skip the pages that did not seem relevant.

The bookmarked portion described an ornate ceremony where a pentagram is painted onto a wooden floor using a horsehair brush dipped in human blood. There was a copper bowl of blood in the center of the pentagram and a smaller silver chalice next to the bowl. The diary did not describe how the blood was obtained.

Hazel Waterhouse describes how she and Bridget recited a long spell in a language she did not recognize. They stripped naked and Hazel unashamedly confessed to her desire to take Bridget into her feather bed and quench their mutual desire. They had kept their love hidden for so long that it was difficult for the author not to reach out to her love when they were naked and alone.

Bridget stood in the middle of the circle and demanded a blade, insisting that it was almost the witching hour. Hazel handed her a silver athame, but Bridget shook her head and pointed to a black box on a wooden dresser. Hazel found the box and opened it, removing a silver sickle with an ornately carved handle.

She walked through the pentagram, taking care not to smudge the lines of blood, and handed the blade to Bridget. Bridget used the blade to cut into her side, drawing blood and filling the silver chalice. Just as the chalice was full, an old clock began to sound the first of twelve bongs.

Bridget reached into the copper bowl and submerged her arm all the way to her shoulder. The bottom of the bowl reached into another dimension. She pulled out a glowing seed the size of an avocado pit and dropped it into the chalice containing her own blood. She explained that in time it would grow into a thorny bush that would produce a fruit that would make them immortal. They took a pie pan from the kitchen, emptied the copper bowl, the silver chalice and the glowing seed into it, and left it by the door.

I read Hazel's account of the aftermath:

> She took my hand and led me down the stairs to the room where we kept the large bed. We were still naked and I was filled with desire. I was aware a woman should not lie down with a woman as if she were a man, but I did

not care. I was in love. I began kissing Bridget's side where she made the cut, tasting the coppery liquid, and worked my way down until my head was between her legs. I used my tongue to pleasure her but my own climax came first. It was difficult to continue while the convulsions of pleasure ran through me. Every part of her instilled passion in me—her looks, her smell, her taste. I had been married before and that marriage produced no passion and no sons. I was content in marriage but never satisfied.

Growing Blood Thorns is a sin. Yet, so was our love. I could not live without it. Bridget demanded so little of me. If she needed my help with a few spells, giving me her body and soul in return, it was a fair trade.

The journal went on to discuss why the seed must be placed outside and that it must stay there overnight. The spirits of the dead, attracted to the blood and the seed, would provide their blessing. After Hazel and Bridget left the bedroom, they spent the night together watching the seed and protecting it until morning.

I skimmed through the rest of the book. Hazel lived an unhappy life in London. Her infant girl was born dead and Hazel was able to produce no other children. Her husband died at a young age of cholera. Hazel found a position as a housekeeper for a wealthy family outside of London.

Her master was a viscount and had money and property but lacked a soul. He was a horrible boss and person. Her first night under his roof she was beaten and raped. He never struck her face, so as not to leave marks his wife would notice. Hazel described herself as having blonde hair and pale skin that bruised easily. And she did not get pregnant—a blessing she had once considered a curse. After her infant daughter died, the midwife had told her she would not be able to have any more children. After a time her master abused her less frequently because a younger girl had joined the household staff. Her employer seemed to have a taste for blonde woman with pale skin because the new hire shared those features. Luckily he preferred the younger woman.

Hazel met Bridget when she was visiting the viscount. She arrived without a male escort and her arrival was kept secret from most of the household to avoid a scandal. Bridget touched Hazel's shoulder as they passed in the hallway and told her that she should not live in fear. No other words were exchanged.

Hazel was informed she would leave with Bridget a week later. She eventually followed her to America. It turned out that Bridget had been hired to perform a spell for her master to destroy a powerful, but distant, member of the royal family. Bridget was willing to forgo payment in exchange for taking Hazel with her.

The book I was reading from was not a Book of Shadows or a Grimoire as I'd expected. It was a memoir. Hazel did not start practicing magic until more than a year after the two women met. The book goes on to chronicle how Hazel was transformed from a beaten-down servant to a powerful witch.

She understood what a horrible spell she had cast. Bridget told her that she cut into her side rather than using her hand or wrist to hide the scar and keep other witches from seeing it. Hazel also confessed how she contributed to finding poor souls in the worst areas of London and bringing them home to the country to feed the Blood Thorns. She never described the killings, focusing instead on how pleased and happy the children seemed to be. They were fed and taken away from the slums. She was able to convince herself that she was doing them a favor. She insisted that the children be allowed to stay for at least a month and be thoroughly spoiled prior to their slaughter. She focused on how they were being freed from a fate worse than a quick and painless death. She never had children and these wretched souls were hers for a time and that was good enough for her. The passages somehow reminded me of the musical *Sweeney Todd*, minus the cannibalism, in that

Hazel felt everything she and Bridget did was justified.

She would gladly kill or die for Bridget. Page after page described their acts of love. Not simply physical acts, although these were included too, but mostly just the simple joyful details of their life together. She described walking through the fields and admiring the stars. She talked about how beautiful and kind Bridget was. She would proclaim her love for Bridget every few pages. In her own words, she was "completely and utterly content."

The journal continued for another fifty pages after the spell was cast. They waited for over a year for the Blood Thorns to mature. The description of Bridget eating the Blood Fruit was disturbing. The skin of the fruit was mostly red with a yellowish tint. The fruit quivered as the silver sickle cut into it. It actually made a noise, "like the gurgling of a baby," when the initial cut was made. The smell of the flesh of the fruit was beyond repulsive. It smelled of "rotten meat and human excrement." The entire inside of the fruit was the color of blood. Black juice poured down Bridget's face as she bit into the flesh.

It was unclear if Hazel ever ate from the fruit. She admitted in her journal that she had little doubt it was evil. She compared it to the fruit consumed by Eve in the Garden of Eden. She said that for a brief moment when she saw Bridget consume the fruit, she considered leaving her. Yet, ultimately, she loved her too much. She also had nowhere else to go.

It was November 1st when they took a ship and headed for America. Bridget had money from selling her magical services to the aristocracy in England but was far from wealthy. She also worried that she would be accused of witchcraft if she remained in England. Although these were enlightened times in London and the big cities, witches were still being burned in the smaller towns and villages.

They told everyone they were sisters. No one suspected them of being lovers when they shared lodgings. Bridget was part of a small coven but did not bring anyone with her to America other than Hazel. She let them know that once she acquired land and money she would send for them. They would create a new world in the heart of America where witches could live in peace. She saw men and women living as equals. She would find a place with fertile earth and few neighbors.

It was not long after their arrival in the States that the journal ended. I wondered what had happened to Hazel. I suspect she would never have voluntarily left Bridget. Her love was unconditional. Since the journal was filled, I suspected another volume existed. I would have loved to find the book but thought it had probably been lost to time. I wondered who had had the good sense to hold on to this one and how it got into Mr. Levi's hands.

I remember reading a novel by Kafka only to discover it was unfinished. I turned to the last page to find the last ten pages were blank. That was how I felt now, unsatisfied, with more questions than answers.

I knew Bridget had married a wealthy landowner. It was possible that Hazel had continued to live with her after the marriage under the ruse that they were sisters. Since Bridget was my client's aunt, I suspected she had no children of her own. At the same time there were no references to a brother or sister.

Being a powerful woman back then would certainly subject a woman to scrutiny. If it were known that she was also a witch and a lesbian, she would not have been tolerated. I was not surprised that there was controversy when her husband died and she inherited the land all around us. Yet she'd managed to create all of this. I couldn't help being impressed. She must have been tired of hiding from the world and needed a place where she could be herself.

The book could be a fake, but I doubted it. The pages felt old, as did the binding. Besides, it would be easier to fake a few pages than a whole book. I wasn't a big fan of Mr. Levi, but he would certainly recognize a fake when he saw it. I also couldn't see him as the perpetrator of a hoax by creating this volume on his own.

Besides, you would have to be a hell of a forger and a writer to fake the feelings contained within these pages. Hazel's love was so exuberant, so all-consuming. Love and empathy jumped off the pages. As a lawyer, I was used to reading and writing briefs and motions, documents without passion. The raw honesty of the text was jarring.

It occurred to me that Mr. Levi had only copied the pages where the ceremony took place to obtain the seed. He had not copied the pages that confirmed the murder of innocents or the eating of the fruit. I hoped he had not read through the entire book. The other parts were far more damning. Yet, the concept of a person tried for the sins of her ancestor was foreign to me.

I closed the book and left the house. I was in no mood to further engage Mr. Levi. I looked down at my watch. I had been reading for two hours. Bridget had to be climbing the walls.

Who knows? Maybe witches could literally climb walls.

CHAPTER TWENTY

~~

WHEN I RETURNED to the house, Bob, Bridget, and Wendy were on the sofa talking. They looked up at me. I could tell from the look on her face that Bridget was annoyed.

"What took you so long?" she said. "We have one day."

I explained the situation with the book. She seemed satisfied. I had to forgive her impatience. The trial was to begin in the morning. It was her life on the line.

"I don't get how a person could be held responsible for what a distant relative did," I said.

"I saw a *Star Trek* episode where Worf was accused of treason based on the acts of his father," Bob said.

"I saw that one as well," I said. I whispered the rest in Bob's ear, "Yet, having the desire to get laid someday, I would never admit to it in front of the fairer sex."

"Not to interrupt, but perhaps we can discuss our plan," Bridget said.

I consulted my notepad. "I thought it would make sense for Wendy to speak with Serena Parker," I said. "She claims that last year, before Samhain, Bridget left a pie pan of blood by her door. I would also like Wendy to speak with Bethany Montgomery, who claims to have heard strange noises coming from your house. My guess is the members of the coven would prefer to speak with one of their own." I took a seat facing the couch. I felt as if I was rallying the troops.

"I have known Serena and Bethany since they were born. I am sure they will cooperate," Wendy said.

"Good," I said, putting a checkmark on my list. "As for Serena, I want to know when she saw this pie pan of blood and how she determined it was blood and not cream, wine, or water. Did she actually go onto the porch and inspect it? Did she taste it? Could there be a rational explanation other than it being blood? Did Bridget leave cream or water out for a stray cat or dog? Could she have been providing wine as a tribute to the spirits? Where was Serena at when she made the observation? At Halloween I replace my white porch light bulb with a back light or an orange bulb. The lighting can cause the color of liquid in a bowl to appear to be a different color. Darkness also causes an absence of color, which means red can look black. What was the lighting like? Who was with her when she saw it? Who did she tell and when? Did she see Bridget put it out or even see her in the house?"

"All right, I get the idea," Wendy said.

"Good, take notes," I said.

"What about Bethany?" Wendy asked.

"Same deal," I said, tapping my pen on my notepad. "I want to know what she heard and saw. I want to know when she heard those noises and who was present. I want to know who she told and when she told them. I am looking for detailed notes."

"What am I going to do?" Bob asked, not looking particularly eager.

"You and I will interview Tim Johnson, who claims to have witnessed Bridget running through the field near the Blood Thorns with a child. We will locate the Amish family he spoke of. Although, if it is the couple we already met, it will not be worth our time. I would like to start by taking another look at the Blood Thorn."

"What shall I do?" Bridget asked. She sat on the edge of the couch, looking eager, soft, and vulnerable, and my heart went out to her.

I thought a moment and made some notes. "I want you to make a list of every member of this coven. I want to know how long you have known them. Who might have an incentive to falsely accuse you of this crime? Who could benefit financially from your death?"

"I should be able to do that," Bridget said, sitting back on the couch again. Her tone was strangely unemotional.

I gave her a long, searching look. "I also want to know what spells can or could be used against you. Could a glamour be used to create a false image of a blood-filled pie pan or a person running with a child? Are there innocent spells or ceremonies that can mimic forbidden ones? I also want to know more about Bridget Bishop. Maybe there is another account of her life other than that of Hazel Waterhouse. I want to know Bridget Bishop's history and any information you have on her use of blood magic."

She made a face. "That should keep me occupied," she said, her tone a bit snarky.

"One more thing," I said, raising an index finger. "I need a tape measure."

Bridget left the room and returned ten minutes later with an old metal twenty-five-foot tape measure. Bob and I walked out the door. With Bob's help I measured the distance from the front porch door to the stairs. As well as the length of the front porch. I also measured from the door to the light bulb. After that I walked around the house, checking the line of sight from the front door.

Afterward Bob and I headed out toward the area of the field that hid the Blood Thorns. It was getting colder. I wore a leather jacket and Bob was wearing a flannel-lined jean jacket.

"Why start here? We have been here already," Bob said.

"We need to see it when the sun is out. I am hoping I will

have more insight than the first time we saw it. Maybe we will have a better idea of what to look for. Besides, this is the scene of the crime. Maybe there is some clue as to what happened that we missed the first time."

Bob paused and walked in a circle, taking a thorough look around him. "There are no fences around here. If we can walk over here, anyone can."

When we got to the edge of the wooded area, Calvin—the Yukon Cornelius lookalike—was waiting for us. He was dressed in jeans, steel-toed boots and the same Carhartt jacket as before.

"I wondered if you two were coming back," he said.

"Have you been here the whole time?" Bob asked.

"No, it is just luck you found me both times. We are taking shifts. Once the thorns produce the fruit it shouldn't be left unwatched."

"Why?" Bob said.

"That kind of power can be a temptation," Calvin said. "Follow me. I will take you to the path."

We walked the same way we had come the last time, but I could feel a change. The air was still and the smell of rot was not as strong.

When we got to the crater with the Blood Thorns in the middle, the plant looked different. It seemed to wrap around itself to protect a yellowish red egg that I knew to be the fruit. If anything, the Blood Thorns seemed smaller.

"The fruit is in the middle," Calvin said.

"Only one?" I said.

"Of course. It is also ripe for only one day, October thirty-first. On November first, the fruit and the plant will die."

"How do you know?" I asked.

"I was told by the elders," Calvin said. "I have never seen one. I thought it was just a story witches tell their children around the campfire. Something to scare them."

"How did everyone find out about it?" I asked.

"Mr. Levi was walking by and smelled it. He recognized it immediately as Blood Thorns and convened a meeting of the elders. That's when Bridget was charged."

"You wouldn't have even recognized it?" I asked.

He shrugged. "How could I? As far as anyone knows there is no one alive who has ever seen the Blood Thorns until now."

Bob and I spent an hour or so just looking around. I had no idea what we were looking for. Perhaps the ripped jacket of the real perpetrator with his name sewed into the inside jacket. Maybe a glass bottle containing a handwritten confession. I decided to use my phone to take pictures as I wandered about the area. Yet, without knowing what to look for, taking photos seemed pointless.

The ground was dry and hard and mostly covered in dead grass. There were no footprints that I noticed. No spilled blood or identifiable fibers to test. I was not surprised. We were outside in a field. Anyone could have walked by or entered. Besides, I had no means to test evidence. In truth most of those CSI shows are bullshit. As a lawyer I am fine with the exaggeration of those shows. It's a good thing if the jury believes that the police have more and better tests at their disposal than they actually do.

Bob and I said goodbye to Calvin and headed back to the house. I thought we might surprise Tim Johnson with an in-person meeting rather than a telephone call. It is harder to get rid of an actual person.

CHAPTER TWENTY-ONE

~~~

T IM JOHNSON LIVED in a small house at the edge of a cornfield. I couldn't tell if it was a double wide mobile home or a modular home. A 1970s Chevrolet pickup was parked on the gravel driveway. A 1970s Harley Davidson from the AMF years stood next to the truck.

We walked up to the house. The screen door was missing the screen, so I knocked on the door through the hole. The man who answered was tall and thin and perhaps in his late sixties. He was wearing a flannel shirt and jeans and smelled of cheap cologne.

"What do you want?" the man asked.

"We are looking for Tim Johnson," I said.

"What fur?" He meant "for," of course.

I pointed toward the village. "Mr. Levi, a man from down the road said you would be testifying in some kind of hearing at the village tomorrow."

"You two friends?" the man asked.

"In a manner of speaking," I said.

"All right then, I'm Tim Johnson. Come on in." Tim beckoned us in with a broad gesture.

The front room had shag carpeting and two worn-out sofas and a lazy boy with a small table next to it. On the table was an old remote control and a drink the color of caramel. What I assumed to be the last non-flat screen television in existence stood against the far wall in a large wooden entertainment center with metal feet. A woven textile wall hanging in the shape of an abstract owl was displayed above the television. All the walls were paneled in fake wood in the style popular in the 1970s. We all had a seat.

"So what can I do for you boys?" Mr. Johnson asked.

"How do you know Mr. Levi?" I asked.

"Known him for years. I do odd jobs around the store and house for him. I built most of them bookshelves in that there store of his."

"Are you good friends?"

He paused, wiped his nose with the back of his hand. "He pays good ... and on time. We don't exactly hang out at the same bars."

"He said you saw a woman run off with a child."

"Yeah," he said. "It was about a year ago. Some woman was running while holding a kid through a cornfield toward a wooded area. Real near the village. Across the road from that fortune teller's house."

"Anyone with you at the time?"

"No, I was alone. On my bike. It must have been close to midnight."

"Had you been drinking?"

"I had a few drinks but I weren't drunk."

"Where were you at when you had the drinks?"

"The Rusty Spoke in Arcola."

"Who were you with at the bar?"

"That was a fucking year ago. I have no idea." Annoyance was creeping into Mr. Johnson's voice.

"Sorry if I am getting too personal," I said, eager to please. "I am just trying to understand what happened."

"Well," he said, scratching his nose, "there ain't a lot to it. I was driving by. Saw a woman and a kid. I stopped the bike but they were gone."

"Could you describe the woman?"

"Tall, long black hair. Looked like the picture Mr. Levi showed me."

"Did he show you more than one picture or just the one?"

"Just the one."

"Were you wearing a helmet or goggles at the time?"

"Nope."

"So you were on the road when you saw her. How far into the field was she?"

"I don't know, fifty feet or so."

"What was she wearing?"

"Long pants and a shirt, I think. Can't be sure. The road ain't lit so I was relying on the bike's headlight."

I made a few notes. "What about a hat or glasses? Did she have a coat on?"

"Sorry, it was a long time ago."

"What about the kid? Was it a boy or girl? How old?"

"I don't know. I was a ways away and it was dark." He wrinkled his nose in concentration. "The kid, if I was to guess, was between five and ten year old."

"No one was there other than the woman and the kid?"

"I don't know. Now that you mention it, there could have been someone else. I saw movement in the trees where they were heading. Then again, it could have been wind or a deer. That is more likely, but I don't know."

I looked him in the eye. "I assume Mr. Levi is going to pay you for your time tomorrow. Since you will be missing other jobs to be there."

He didn't hesitate. "Twenty bucks an hour."

"One other question. Why didn't you call the police at the time?"

"The kid weren't bleeding or crying. Seemed odd but no big deal. Why is everyone so interested?"

"Didn't Mr. Levi say?"

He shook his head vigorously. "Nope, and it ain't none of my business. As far as I know there are no missing kids. It was probably the kid's mom taking a late night stroll."

"So was she carrying the child or was he or she walking?"

"It has been so long, I just can't remember for sure."

"Bob, can you think of anything else you want to ask Mr. Johnson?" I asked.

"Nope," Bob said.

"Can I give you some advice?" Mr. Johnson asked.

"Sure."

"It weren't no big deal. Let it go."

"Thanks, we will get out of your hair," I said.

"Do you mind if I take a quick look at your bike?" Bob said. "That's a Harley FX Superglide from the 1970s."

"You know your bikes," Mr. Johnson said with a gap-toothed grin. "It's a 1971. Do you ride?"

"I have an old Indian from the 1950s, but it has been rebuilt so many times I don't know if it still counts as an Indian. By the way, is this the same bike you were driving when you saw that woman?"

"Yep, now you look at it all you want. Before you go, I got a joke for you." He led them outside.

"All right," Bob said.

"What's the difference between Beer Nuts and deer nuts?"

"What?" Bob and I answered together.

"Beer Nuts are ninety-nine cents and deer nuts are under a buck," Mr. Johnson said, slapping his thigh and laughing heartily at his own joke.

Mr. Johnson headed into the house, still laughing, as Bob made a thorough inspection of the bike. I did not interrupt him with questions but instead got into the car. After a few moments he joined me.

"What is with the bike?" I asked.

"It has no fairing or windscreen and it is customized, so the rider sits way back. I believe the dude, but at night, without a helmet or goggles, he wouldn't have had a great view. Also, those old style headlights aren't great."

"Do you think he was drunk?" I asked.

"At the time he saw the woman or now?" Bob asked, answering my question with a question.

"Yes," I said.

"Yes, probably, if I had to guess. I don't think he was lying though."

"I agree."

"Maybe we should head to that bar in Tuscola and ask around?" Bob asked.

"That was a year ago," I said, "and we don't have a specific date. Seems like a waste of time but we could try."

"All that talk of Beer Nuts put me in the mood for bar food," Bob said.

The drive to Arcola was not long but the trip seemed a waste of time. Arcola is the home of the Broom Corn Festival. Its other claim to fame is that it is the birthplace of Johnny Gruelle, the creator of Raggedy Ann and Andy. Apparently it was also the home of The Rusty Spoke.

The bar was not hard to locate. It was a small building with parking in front reserved for motorcycles. This was made clear by an orange and black sign with a picture of a bike that said, "Reserved for motorcycles. All others will have their asses kicked."

We parked around the corner and walked in. The tavern was cool and dark. There was a large bar with a brass rail along the bottom for your feet and nine empty bar stools. There was a mirror behind the bar. At the far end was a regulation-sized pool table that took up about a third of the place and three other tables for seating. Most of the light came from three neon beer signs and dim lighting behind the bar.

There was only one other customer, a large man with a beard and mustache and long frizzy hair tied back in a ponytail. He was wearing jeans and a leather vest with no shirt, revealing multiple tattoos. He sat at a table alone.

"Can I help you boys?" I looked up to see the bartender. He looked to be in his forties with a shaved head and a red beard. He had a deep scar underneath one eye that I did my best to ignore.

"Do you have a menu?" Bob asked.

"Nope, but I can tell you what we've got," he said, hands on hips.

"Do you mind?" I asked.

He ticked the choices off on his fingers. "Cheeseburger, hamburger, grilled cheese, BLT, fries, fried mushrooms, pickled herring, chili, and dill pickles."

"I will have a cheeseburger and fried mushrooms with a Budweiser to wash it down," Bob said.

"I will have a cheeseburger as well," I said. "What type of cheese do you have?"

"Muenster, cheddar, Swiss, blue cheese, provolone, and American," the bartender said. "Except we're out of everything but American."

"American would be good," I said quickly. "Fries and a Coke would be nice too."

He poured our drinks and left to go in back and prepare the food. Obviously this place didn't do much business during the day. Fifteen minutes later he put the food in front of us.

"Do you know a guy named Tim Johnson?" I asked the bartender.

"Sure, he was an elected member of the U.S. House of Representatives until he retired in 2012. He loved this place. He always got the cheeseburger, same as you."

"Another Tim Johnson," Bob said. "Rides a 1971 FX Superglide. Tall, in his sixties."

"Boys," the bartender said, "aren't those the best fucking burgers in the whole word?"

I took a bite. "Yummy," I said.

"Good answer, but I eat this shit too. People don't come here for the food or the ambiance. They come here because they know I don't talk to anyone about anyone. Neither does anyone else who comes here. So eat your fucking burgers. Tip big and get the fuck out."

I heard a noise from behind us and turned to see the large bearded man stand up. The bartender signaled him to sit back down. I decided it was a good time to eat my burger and get out.

Fifteen minutes later we paid our bill and left. I took his advice and tipped generously. Bob looked contemplative.

"What are you thinking?" I asked Bob when we got to the car.

"I can't believe I am saying this, but that may have been the best fucking burger in the world," Bob said.

"It was particularly fresh, thick, and juicy," I agreed.

"I think the bun was homemade as well," Bob said.

"Yes, and mine had a mustard horseradish sauce that was amazing," I added.

"I think I could pass a lie detector test if I was asked, 'Was that the best fucking burger in the whole word,' " Bob said.

"Me too. Although lie detector tests are not admissible in court because they are not reliable," I said.

He blinked. "Are truth spells reliable?"

"I don't know, but it would be hard to move for a Frye Test."

"Is that like when you go to McDonald's, Burger King, and Wendy's and decide who can fry up the best tasting spud?"

"No, it's a test to determine if scientific evidence is admissible in court. I think the test is based on the case, *Frye v. The United States*, and actually concerned a polygraph test. Anyway, the evidence must be generally accepted by the scientific community before being admissible. Most states don't use Frye anymore but Illinois still does."

"My guess is that a truth spell is generally considered reliable among the witchcraft-using community."

"I agree."

"Are we going to check out the last address, the Amish family?" Bob asked.

"If it's the family we already visited it's a waste of time," I said. "We will drive by and find out."

"I will use my phone to get GPS directions."

CHAPTER TWENTY-TWO

~~

IT TURNED OUT the Amish family was indeed the same one we had spoken with earlier. Since there was nothing more to be learned from them and I didn't want to get shot, we decided not to attempt a second interview. I was curious how Mr. Levi was able to talk with them and how he intended to obtain their testimony.

We returned to Bridget's house and found Bridget and Wendy sitting in the parlor. Bridget was holding both of Wendy's hands. Wendy was shaking and seemed far more anxious than Bridget.

"What is going on?" I asked.

"Wendy thinks I am going to die," Bridget said.

"We can't live forever but I would prefer it if you lived past Halloween," I said.

Bridget rose to her feet. "Why don't we go to the kitchen?" she said. "I will make some food, coffee, and tea."

We returned to the kitchen, where Wendy, Bob, and I sat at the table. Bridget made herself busy in the kitchen. Wendy seemed agitated. I don't know if it was because she was generally afraid for Bridget or if she had learned something new from Serena Parker or Bethany Montgomery.

Something smelled good and I turned around to see that

Bridget was cooking dinner. She was unaware that Bob and I had just eaten at the bar. Neither of us mentioned it.

"I hope you all like shepherd's pie and pumpkin soup," Bridget said.

"That sounds great," Bob said with a genuine enthusiasm that seemed odd, given he had just eaten.

"Looking forward to it," I lied.

"So, what did you boys find out?" Bridget asked.

I shared with Wendy and Bridget what we learned. I skipped the entire episode at the bar, of course. They both seemed interested. Wendy recoiled when I talked about the Blood Thorns, as if she had not believed they existed until that moment.

"Wendy," I said, picking up my notepad, "tell me about what Ms. Parker said."

"She was glad to see me at first, but it was clear she did not want to talk about it. She said it occurred around this same time of year last fall. She remembered the Samhain celebration had ended that day or at least near that date. She said it was just after midnight and she was walking around. She couldn't sleep. That was when she saw it. She went up to the porch and said she could feel the evil emanating from that pie pan. She was sure it was filled with blood."

"Was anyone with her?" I asked.

"No."

"Did she inspect it closely or put her finger in it?"

"No, she was afraid."

"Was Bridget in the house at the time?"

"I didn't ask her that."

"Was there a porch light on?"

"She wasn't sure."

"Who did she tell about it? If she felt it was evil, did she tell someone back then?" I asked.

"She said she'd never told anyone until she found out almost a year later that Bridget was being charged with growing Blood Thorns," Wendy said.

"What about Ms. Montgomery?"

Wendy sighed. "She claims she has heard strange noises coming from this house over the years. Some could have been the screams of children or the cries of babies."

"Could she give dates and times when these noises occurred?" I asked.

"Mostly late at night. She could not be specific as to dates and times. She said she is an insomniac and is up at all hours of the night."

"Did she go to the police or anyone else at the time she first heard the noises? Could it have been the television or radio?"

"I didn't ask about the television or radio. She didn't do anything or tell anyone until the charges came up. She claims she was afraid of Bridget."

"Why did she claim to be afraid of Bridget?"

Wendy started to tear up. "She would not say."

"Did they both seem like they were being truthful?"

"Yes," Wendy said with particular vehemence.

"It's your turn, Bridget," I said. Wendy seemed to be weeping silently. "Why would Bethany Montgomery fear you and lie about you? Why would Serena Parker?"

"I don't know. Perhaps it is because my land would go to the coven when I die. Everyone would benefit," Bridget said.

"Would Bethany Montgomery or Serena Parker know that?" I asked.

"I am unaware who would know, other than Wendy and Mr. Levi," Bridget said.

"I want to work in the library tonight," I said. "I need that list of people in the coven and why they might lie about you. Also, please pull any books from the shelves you found by or about Bridget Bishop."

Bridget finished chopping onions and dried her hands. No tears for her. Perhaps she was not sensitive to onions. "I am done with the list," she said. "I found one book in the library written by Bridget Bishop. I remember there being more, but that was all I could find. I will have it for you after dinner. There may be other books that mention her but I have had no luck locating them."

"I want to go over your testimony," I said as she continued to combine ingredients. "We may also want to have Wendy testify concerning your reputation for honesty in the community."

Bridget stood a little straighter and said, "I do not want to waste the time of the coven. My reputation as to all things is known by the entire village."

"We don't have to decide tonight," I said, putting up a hand to placate her. "We can wait until the close of their case before determining who to call as our witnesses."

The meal was a somber affair. I felt the connection between Wendy and Bridget as they seemed to look into each other. They appeared to understand something I could not fathom. Since Bob and I had both eaten earlier, I was not terribly hungry. I assumed Bridget took my lack of appetite as concern for her predicament rather than a statement about her cooking. Although shepherd's pie and pumpkin soup are not among my favorite foods.

It was not the food itself I did not like. It was the memories surrounding it. At my grade school they used to serve shepherd's pie once a week. It brought back unhappy memories of being called "Sam I am" or "Samwich" by the pigtailed monster known as Becky.

"How often does this happen?" Bob asked, playing with his mashed potatoes.

"Does what happen?" Wendy said.

"How often do they have hearings to determine if the coven rules have been broken? How many people have been burned alive?"

It was a good question that I had not thought to ask. In fact, if these types of allegations were made a lot, there had to be a record of what occurred. Even if it was not a precedent, it would provide a greater understanding of the process.

"Never," Wendy said. "This would be the first such hearing since the coven came to America."

I was taken aback. "No one has ever broken a rule of the coven?" I asked.

"Not one of the central tenets," Wendy said. "Not a spell or ritual related to blood. Well, maybe they have, but no one has been accused of it or tried."

"That is not good," I said.

"Why?" Bridget said.

"Because it means the people judging you know that the coven doesn't frivolously charge witches of such offenses. The rarity of the situation will also make the act seem even more egregious. This is a tough case. We know that Blood Thorns have been grown. We know people have died. Our argument is not that nothing happened, only that Bridget did not do it. Remember, no one else is on trial. Bridget is the only person they can convict. If they are outraged enough about the act itself, they may find her guilty because there is no one else."

"These people know me," Bridget said emphatically. "I believe they will be fair."

"Well, I don't know them," I said, finally putting my fork down in defeat. "Yet, if *they* believe you are putting the coven at risk, they might act unpredictably."

"It is too late to worry of such things," Bridget said.

"I will set up in the library," I said, standing. "I will keep quiet because I know your bedroom is right next door."

"I doubt I will sleep at all tonight, but if I do, I will sleep on the second floor. I rarely use the third floor bedroom," Bridget said.

I was about to leave for the library when Bridget brought out a large apple crisp and some pumpkin pie for dessert. There was also whipped cream that tasted and smelled of amaretto. I sat down again. She offered brandy and port as after dinner drinks, but everyone had work to do and selected tea and coffee instead.

When we finished, Bob and I headed to the library.

Bridget did not want to go over her testimony. I didn't argue, given that the testimony would change after we heard the case against her. It was going to be a long night.

CHAPTER TWENTY-THREE

~~~

A FTER BOB RETRIEVED his laptop, we headed up to the third floor. The library was how I'd left it. I took a seat at the oak table while Bob wandered around, stopping in front of the oil painting of Bridget Bishop.

"I see why you are willing to do so much for Bridget," he said, his eyes popping out of his head. "She is even more beautiful naked. Not overly modest, though, if she'd display a painting like this."

"That is not Bridget Gillis," I said, "but her great-great aunt, Bridget Bishop."

He stared for a long moment before saying, "That is hard to believe. They are indistinguishable."

I pointed. "Look at the date on the painting."

Bob examined the date and the signature and took a closer look at the paint and the frame. After a few minutes he said, "The painting is definitely old. The varnish is yellowing and there is a lot of dirt and grime, but it still seems impossible. The resemblance is uncanny. Yet, her body is amazing."

"I can't believe you are ogling my girlfriend's naked picture and her perfect form," I said. As I said the word "girlfriend," I couldn't help but wonder if I could really call her that. We'd only been together once.

"It's not her body but that of her aunt," Bob said, slightly peeved, "and she is not perfect."

"I don't know," I said, putting my hands palm down on the table and leaning back. "What is more disrespectful, the ogling or the negative critique?"

"She has a slight scar along the side of her stomach." He traced it with his finger. "A line of darker pigmentation. I am not sure if it is an old injury or a mistake by the artist."

I heard what he was saying and had an epiphany. No—perhaps that is too strong a word—I had a sudden realization. That scar could have been made by the curved silver blade mentioned in Hazel Waterhouse's journal. This was further proof of Ms. Bishop's guilt. Yet, Bridget Bishop was not on trial. I told Bob about what I had read.

Bob was about to comment when the library door opened. Wendy walked in, carrying a tray with two mugs, a pot of coffee, and a pot of tea along with flat English tea biscuits. Bridget was behind her with a notebook and an old leather book in her hand. Bridget and Wendy placed the items on the table.

"I forgot I had this book downstairs," Bridget said. "It was written by Bridget Bishop. The notebook lists each member of the coven and what I know of them."

"Thanks," I said.

"Stay here as long as you like," she said. "We won't bother you again. I have many prayers and spells to perform."

"Prayers and spells to help us win the trial?" Bob asked.

She pursed her lips and gave a brisk shake of her head. "Magic should not be used for such purposes. I only seek a fair trial and to ensure that justice is done."

"All right," I said, picking up the book. "I will go through the list and this book. Let me know if you want to go over your testimony."

"I want to hear their evidence first. Once they are done, we will have another night to decide what evidence we wish to present."

The look I gave her was probably reproachful. "This is the first time you have said that."

"Sorry," she said, "I assumed you knew. Although I guess I had no reason to make such an assumption."

"What if their evidence can't be presented in one day?" I asked.

"It will be. They will go until midnight if necessary, but it will not come to that."

"How do you know?"

"We know the witnesses they intend to call. There is no reason they can't complete their case in one session. If you need me for something else, feel free to ring the bell. I can hear it from anywhere in the house. It is said to be charmed by the first school teacher in the village."

"What bell?" I asked.

Bridget walked over to a bookcase, removed a large brass school bell with a long black handle, and placed it on the table next to me. I hadn't noticed the bell earlier.

"Listen," she said, leaning closer to me, "don't stay up too late. I want you fresh for the trial. I also want to thank you." She bent down and gave me a gentle kiss on the lips. It was our first physical contact since making love. I could feel the electricity pass between us. Bridget and Wendy left the room.

When the door closed, Bob gave me a long look. There was something bothering him, but he couldn't decide whether to say it aloud. "So what is the plan?" he finally said. I had no doubt that he was avoiding what was really on his mind.

"I'm sure it's a waste of time, but can you go through the list of villagers and Google each person? See if we can find information on anyone."

Bob opened his laptop. "What are you going to do?" he asked.

"I intend to read Bridget Bishop's book. I also want to review what we have learned so far and prepare cross-examination of the named witnesses. Although I don't know what the rules are."

"What do you mean?"

"In court you generally ask leading questions in cross-examination and open-ended questions for direct. I don't know how to handle this."

"What is the difference?"

"An open-ended question might be, 'What is the weather like?' A leading question would be 'It is raining out, isn't it?' "

"I understand."

"I don't." I slapped the table for emphasis. "If truth spells work, then who cares about any of it? It seems to me the purpose of a trial is to ferret out the truth. If we can know the truth just by asking the question, then who cares about the rules of procedure?"

Bob frowned. "Isn't that a good thing?"

"I'm not sure. If truth spells work, then why not place one on Bridget? Then she could deny the allegations and we are done. She could prove her innocence."

"Why don't you ask her?"

"I will. I'm not sure I like the idea of switching the burden of proof to a defendant. I know I don't believe in an infallible truth spell."

Bob laughed. "You're just afraid it will put you out of a job."

"Yes," I said wryly, "I will never work before a witches' tribunal again."

Bob began going through the list of people living in the village, running each of their names through a Google search. I suspected he would be spending a lot of time sifting through unrelated people with the same name.

I have Googled my own name. There is a rock musician and an actor named Sam Roberts along with a politician and a journalist. None of them has anything to do with me other than the name.

I picked up the book written by Bridget Bishop, excited by the prospect of reading it. Perhaps it would continue the story started by Hazel Waterhouse. I was oddly curious about what happened after their arrival in America.

I was immediately disappointed. It was not a narrative—more like a recipe book. There were mundane spells related to losing weight and making thicker gravy. Spells to help you sleep and to reduce bloating. There were also more exciting spells related to flying and projection of illusion. You could manipulate your dreams and those of others with a few words and some herbs and spices. There was an entire section on counter-spells. Spells that could keep a witch from being spelled, thus allowing a curse or other spell to bounce off the witch with no ill effects. The writing covered only one side of each sheet, leaving the other side blank.

There was a list of potions, and along with each potion a list of ingredients, from Agrimony to Za'atar. Not just herbs, but less culinary choices such as insects and animal blood. Luckily human blood did not appear to be a mainstream ingredient.

A spell or potion could help alleviate almost every problem in life. There was a spell for acne as well as one to help enhance your love life. That spell did not include a warning about erections lasting four hours or more. There were spells related to more serious difficulties as well, from cancer to zygomycosis, which is a fungal infection caused by bread mold.

If these spells could perform as advertised, doctors and pharmaceutical companies would be obsolete overnight. The book certainly suggested that the lifespan of a witch could be much longer than that of an ordinary person. That said, I was unsure of its significance for this trial.

I was interested in a couple of things. One was that the first page and the cover both had a large I on them. I did not know if that was the Roman numeral I—implying there would be additional volumes—or something else. The last page also caught my eye. It was a list of things that I assumed were spells but not included in this volume:

1. Summoning the Guardians of the Watchtowers
2. Blood Spells

3. Creatures of Darkness and Creatures of Light

4. Blood Potions

5. Spells of Clairvoyance

6. Love Spells

7. Spells to Open Gates

Below the list of spells was a hand-drawn candle that looked like three separate candles braided together, along with a sketch of a lemon or lime.

In addition to this sketch on the last page of the book, there were what seemed to be randomly placed sketches of symbols and objects throughout. Many of the sketches were signs of the Tarot. Others were visual depictions of herbs and other ingredients for potions.

I spent two hours going through the book and was rewarded with nothing I could use. I then decided to make a list of each witness named by Mr. Levi and write a list of key questions I wanted to ask. As I started the questions, Bob interrupted me.

"Dude, there is nothing of any use here," Bob said.

"Nothing?" I asked.

"Apparently this village of witches and warlocks doesn't publish much on the Internet."

"Thanks for trying. Why don't you get some sleep? Tomorrow is a big day."

He closed his laptop, tucked it under his arm, and stood. "Cool, but don't stay up too late yourself."

"Give me another hour and I am going to hit the hay as well."

"I know you're not asking," he said, looking around, "but if you were to ask me if this place gives me the willies, then the answer would be yes."

"Could be worse," I said. "Could be the heebie-jeebies or the screaming meemies."

"I think the willies are worse than the others," Bob said.

I stood up and stretched my legs. "I would vote for screaming meemies," I said, "but I would stipulate that it's subjective."

"*Stipulate*? You sound like a fucking lawyer," Bob said.

"I would prefer the heebie-jeebies, the willies, and the screaming meemies combined as opposed to explosive diarrhea," I said.

Bob shrugged. "Who wouldn't? But that's random. What has diarrhea to do with anything?"

"Sorry," I said. "I'm tired and feeling erratic."

" 'Night, dude."

" 'Night."

After Bob left, I began writing questions. I felt so out of my depth that I needed an oxygen tank. I couldn't allow for Bridget to be put to death. Two hours passed before my thoughts no longer made sense to myself. I wandered down to my room. I gathered my bathrobe, tooth brush, and tooth paste and walked to the bathroom, where I brushed my teeth and took a shower. The cold water did nothing to clear my head.

CHAPTER TWENTY-FOUR

~~~

I WAS EXHAUSTED, but somehow sleep refused to come. I vaguely remembered a sleep potion in Bridget Bishop's book. Although, if memory served, it required mandrake root, wormwood, and basil as well as a cauldron and an hour's prep time.

My eyes opened. I was sitting in a wooden chair before a large stone fireplace. The interior of the house was wood framed and simple. On a small wooden table next to me stood a whale oil lamp, but other than that, the fire in the fireplace provided the only illumination in the room. Across from me, on a similar chair, sat Cotton Mather, wearing clothing this time. He was heavyset with long gray hair parted down the middle. Around his neck was a white ruff that looked like a short scarf. He wore a white shirt, a black waistcoat, dark knee breeches, white stockings, and black buckled shoes.

"I see you have left the shower at the supermarket in favor of a house," I said.

"Yes, it is a little more my style," Cotton Mather said.

"Are you here to tell me something?" I asked.

He spread his arms, palms up, as if in welcome. "It is your dream," he replied.

"That is not an answer. Besides, I only know your name from

the Salem Witch Trials. What can you contribute?"

He made a steeple with his hands. "What do you know about the Salem Witch Trials?"

"I know they began in 1692 in Salem, Massachusetts. A group of young ladies accused older women of witchcraft. These trials were also synonymous with injustice."

"How do you know there was an injustice?"

"First of all," I said, "witches don't exist. Second of all, there was no real proof."

"Witches do exist," he said simply. "You are in a village full of witches. You have seen enough to know that witches exist."

"Yes, I guess I do now."

He inclined his head. "I would agree that those tried and killed were not witches. Even if they were witches, that would be no excuse. Witches are people like anyone else; some are good and some are bad. The claims we made in Salem as to the ties those women had with the Devil were equally false." He pulled out a long-stemmed clay pipe and filled it with tobacco. He looked awfully solid for a ghost. I wondered if he was actually going to light the pipe.

"I see," I said.

"I was puritanical and ignorant but not evil," he went on. "I believed in what we were doing. I believed in the devil and in witchcraft. I believed that those alleged victims of witchcraft, mostly innocent women and girls, were telling the truth. I further believed that they believed their allegations. We acted out of fear and ignorance but not malevolence." He finally lit the pipe with a long wooden match.

"Despite the motivation, it was still wrong," I said.

"People are mostly good," he said, "except when they act out of fear."

"I am not sure I believe that," I said. "Those 'witches' put you in no danger. If they were a threat, they would have destroyed their prosecutors and tormentors with their powers during these 'trials.' "

He nodded. "Hindsight, through modern eyes, paints another picture. I got caught up in the emotions of the moment. I want to make amends and make sure it never happens again."

I went on, "I am also not convinced people are good. Slavery and the persecution and murder of Native Americans were motivated by money and greed. As are war and genocide. I would argue fear may have been a motivation but not the only one."

Cotton Mather puffed vigorously on his pipe before responding. "I was genuinely afraid of the devil and of witches," he said. "For that matter I genuinely feared the Indians. You were not alive during the Indian wars of the seventeenth century. You did not live in a world where science was in its infancy and death was a daily occurrence. Salem was on the edge of the world and the world was terrifying."

"You are correct," I said. "I have no right to pass judgment on you. The Salem Witch Trials occurred at another time in another world. Which leads me to my next point: what does it have to do with me and my current situation? Why are you here?"

"I am here to help. I told you I want to make amends for my past misdeeds. Either that or it is just one of those strange random dreams."

"Fine, I can use all the help I can get," I said. "I'm not Ebenezer Scrooge and you are not a spirit. I won't attribute your presence to undigested meat or potatoes. Although that shepherd's pie was a bit dodgy. What are your ideas?"

He leaned forward for emphasis and stared me straight in the eyes. "Witches and warlocks recall the Salem Witch Trials with horror. You may be able to discredit evidence by comparing it to the evidence presented at those trials."

"Such as …?"

He paused for a moment as smoke filled the room. I could smell the rich scent of tobacco. I wondered if people were supposed to be able to detect odors in their dreams.

"There were some odd techniques used in Salem that will not be relevant. No one will try to force a confession from Bridget by torture—pressing, dunking, or submersion in water."

"Is that why they won't force her to agree to a truth spell? A forced confession, even by spell, is troubling because of the Salem Witch Trials?"

"Yes. Most people in the community feel it is wrong to force a confession. That and some witches have been known to deflect a truth spell. A truth spell can be avoided if you are a practiced and powerful witch or warlock. Bridget is considered a very powerful witch. There are other tests as well that have no validity and will of course not be used. For example, forcing a witch to say the Lord's Prayer without error or using a needle to see if they bleed."

"I am a bit lost here."

"Have you heard of Spectral Evidence?" he asked.

"No."

"During the witch trials in Salem the prosecutors were allowed to present evidence such as dreams and visions. I was actually against the use of said evidence on principle but I do confess to having used it before. Chief Justice William Stoughton had no qualms about introducing this type of evidence."

"That is crazy."

"It is and it is not. A witch actually can enter a person's dreams. Yet, it would be unusual. A witch can also project images and visions by using a glamour spell."

"I see."

"Of course Mr. Levi will use eyewitness testimony as they did in the Salem Witch Trials. I would remind the trier of fact how ineffective that was in Salem. Innocent women were put to death based on eyewitness testimony. They may also seek to search Bridget's home and other places for artifacts related to the crime. Another technique used in the witch trials."

"How does it help us to remind the trier of fact about the witch trials in Salem?"

"Think about it. If this trial is about Mr. Levi and his use of questionable evidence and techniques rather than about Bridget, you have won. Play on their emotions, make this out to be a new witch hunt using the methods of the past."

"You want me to appeal to the passions and prejudices of the trier of fact. A lawyer is not allowed to do that."

He smiled, showing what was clearly a set of wooden dentures. "You are not her lawyer. You are an advocate. You must do that." Each time he said "you," he pointed a finger in my direction.

"I am not sure I want to take advice from you. Your credibility is a little tarnished. Your legal experience comes from prosecuting innocent people and putting them to death."

"You need to trust me," he said gravely. "Bridget needs you. It is also well known even in the planes of the dead that Bridget makes a lovely shepherd's pie."

"Huh?"

He stood from his chair, walked over to me, and placed a hand under my chin. It felt oddly furry.

I awoke to find Bridget's black cat on my chest. A paw was resting beneath my chin. I began to adjust to being awake. I could smell coffee and cinnamon rolls. I put on my robe and headed down to the breakfast table.

Chapter Twenty-Five

~~~

As I walked into the kitchen I realized I was the only person not dressed. Wendy wore a long green linen dress, black tights, and black shoes. Her blonde hair was tied back in a braided ponytail. Bridget was dressed in black, her black hair pulled into a bun. She wore little or no makeup and looked like a really good-looking school teacher. It was the perfect image to present for this hearing—conservative and innocent. Even Bob looked good, with khaki pants, a blue sports coat, a white button down shirt, and a Jerry Garcia tie.

"Good morning," Bridget said as I walked into the kitchen.

"I was worried about you," Bob said. "Bridget had to send the cat up to wake you."

"What time is it?" I asked, looking for a wall clock. "My fluffy alarm clock didn't say."

"No alarm clock is purrrfect," Bob said.

"It is six in the morning," Bridget said, handing me a plate with two scrambled eggs and a rib eye steak. "We need to get ready."

There were rolls, biscuits, and muffins in a basket on the table. There was also hot sauce, marmalade, and apple butter. Bridget must have been up early to make all of this.

I sat down with my plate. Without asking, Wendy brought

me a glass of orange juice and some hot tea. Everything felt oddly domestic, given we were going to be at trial.

Bob seemed unaffected by what was about to happen. Wendy, however, was visibly shaken. Like Bob, Bridget seemed oddly calm. I was starting to get nervous, but I tried to appear professional.

We ate in relative silence. It was clear everyone was waiting on me, but now that I was here I had nothing to say. I decided it was not worth the effort to make conversation.

I was not hungry and as a result the food was without flavor and Bridget's efforts were wasted. My mind fought to stay with me rather than wander ahead. I did not wish to risk trying to function on an empty stomach, so I ate most of what was on my plate. Afterward I excused myself to shower and dress. As I looked in the mirror, an older man stared back at me. There were new lines on my face, as well as further graying around the temples.

Although I looked good for a man in his thirties, I no longer had the energy I once had. This hearing was going to take a lot out of me. That was particularly true if it resulted in the death of the woman I loved.

I put on a black suit, a white shirt, and a Christian Lacroix tie. If not for the bright yellow tie and the lack of facial hair, I appeared almost Amish. I also put on my watch, a Jaeger-LeCoultre Reverso, obtained from a man I'd sent to hell. After all, he wouldn't need it where he was going. Mr. Smart had had good taste, despite his shortcomings. I put my notes and Ms. Bishop's book in a brown leather briefcase.

Everyone was ready to go by the time I walked down the stairs. As we headed across the field to the community center, we joined other villagers—some ahead of us, some behind. No one was going to miss the show.

The furniture in the community center had been rearranged since the last time we were here. On the stage were three long tables. The tables formed a triangle, with two closer to the audience and the third closer to the back of the room. Between the three tables was a lone empty chair. Bob, Bridget, and I sat at one table with our backs to the assembled villagers. Wendy joined the audience.

Twenty minutes later, Mr. Levi took a seat at the other table with his back to the crowd. Finally the three remaining elders took a seat at the table farthest back, facing the villagers. They wore black robes like actual judges. On their table sat two large crystals, a candle, and five hour glasses of various sizes. The people stood as the elders entered the room. For a long moment the room was silent.

Finally Glenda LeFay spoke. "Mr. Levi, are you prepared to go forward?"

Mr. Levi stood and said, "I am."

"Mr. Roberts?"

"Yes." I followed Mr. Levi's lead and stood.

"You may begin." Glenda turned over an hour glass.

"I would ask to call Serena Parker," Mr. Levi said.

I stood, interrupting him. "Is there no opportunity for an opening statement?"

"No, there is not," Ms. LeFay said in a flat voice.

"Can I move to exclude witnesses?"

"If that is your request, then it is denied," Ms. LeFay said.

Serena Parker was short and in her twenties. She wore a black skirt and a silky white blouse. Her mousy brown hair was tied back with a black ribbon. She looked about as happy as a pig on slaughter day.

Serena sat in the chair in the center of the three tables. Her entire body was shaking. She never looked up, her eyes fixed on the floor.

"Do you consent?" Ms. LeFay asked Serena.

"Yes," she whispered, her voice almost inaudible.

Mr. Levi stood and retrieved a crystal from the table of the elders. He walked over to the witness and handed it to her.

She took it in both hands and said, "I pray to the gods and

goddesses of the sky to take my breath should I lie. I will give up my life and choose to die."

"Blessed be," the villagers said in one voice.

The crystal glowed a deep green. The elders seemed satisfied. Mr. Levi held up a small notebook. I opened my briefcase and handed a legal pad and pen to Bridget and Bob.

"If you have a question or comment, pass me a note," I whispered to Bridget and Bob.

"Ms. Parker, how do you know Bridget Gillis?"

"We are sister witches of this coven. I have lived here my entire life. Bridget's mother left the coven and the house stood empty. Bridget moved back maybe ten years ago. She has been a friend, a sister, and a neighbor for the last ten years."

"I want to draw your attention to about a year ago. What did you see?"

"It was late, maybe two in the morning, and I was walking around. I remember it was on or near Samhain. As I walked past Bridget's house, I saw a pie pan full of blood by her front door."

"Objection," I said, "call for speculation. How does she know it was full of blood? There has been no foundation."

"Mr. Roberts, this is not a court of law," Ms. LeFay said with steel in her voice. "We are civilized. Let her talk. When she is done, you can ask your questions."

"He can ask them now. I am done," Mr. Levi said.

"Mr. Roberts, you may ask your questions," Ms. LeFay said.

"Ms. Parker, who were you with at the time you saw this pie pan of alleged blood?" I asked.

"I was alone."

"You had consumed alcohol during Samhain, had you not?"

"I think I did. I wasn't drunk or anything. I believe there was pumpkin and apple ale at the celebration. I am not a big drinker. There was mulled wine as well."

"That night you had consumed some ale and wine."

"Yes, I think so."

"You would agree it was dark at two in the morning?"

"Yes."

"You never went onto the porch, did you? I mean you never sought permission from Ms. Gillis to go onto her porch?"

"No, I was on the grass."

"How far away from the porch were you when you observed this?"

"It was a year ago. I can't remember."

"You could have been twenty feet away, is that correct?"

She paused in concentration. "I was closer than that."

"Ten feet?"

She shrugged. "I can't remember."

"You would agree that Ms. Gillis's porch is ten feet wide and the door is ten feet from the edge of the porch?"

She shook her head, helplessly. "I don't know."

"You could have been an additional ten feet from the edge of the porch, is that correct?"

"I don't know."

"Ms. Gillis only has one light on her porch, at least three feet from the door."

"I don't remember."

"You also don't remember the color of the bulb, do you?"

"No."

"You were concerned because a pie pan of blood is disturbing, isn't it?"

"Yes, of course. It's blood magic. Blood can be used to feed evil spirits or worse yet, feed Blood Thorns."

"That is why you immediately contacted the elders and called the police. It was a serious threat to the community."

"No I didn't, not at the t-time," she said with a slight stutter.

"You in fact waited almost a year before telling anyone. Until you heard about these charges."

"I couldn't be sure, and Bridget was a sister witch."

"You also didn't want to be sure. You never touched the blood, did you?

"No."

"For all you know it was mulled wine, isn't that true?"

Her brow knit in confusion. "Why would someone put mulled wine in a pie pan in front of their door?"

"Objection, that is non-responsive. I would move to strike."

"Mr. Roberts, this is not a court of law," Ms. LeFay said.

"You never touched the substance?"

"No."

"Smelled it?"

"No."

"Tasted it?"

"No."

"Examined it under light?"

"No."

"Has Ms. Gillis ever read your fortune?"

"Sure, she has read almost everyone's."

"Has she ever told you anything you did not like?"

"I guess."

"You have spoken with Mr. Levi a number of times before today about this, haven't you?"

"Yes, well I spoke with him about three weeks ago at a community meeting when he explained what Bridget had done. I also spoke with him last night to go over what I was going to say."

"How long have you known Mr. Levi?"

"Most of my life."

"Good friends?"

"He has been more of a mentor, an elder."

I looked to Bob and Bridget. It was clear they had nothing to add.

"No further questions."

"Mr. Levi?" Ms. LeFay asked.

"You believed it was blood didn't you?" Mr. Levi said.

"Objection, he has already asked this question. Besides, a truth spell has been cast."

"I agree with Mr. Roberts," Ms. LeFay said. "Let us keep moving forward. Shall we, Mr. Levi?"

Mr. Levi nodded. "Then I have no further questions. I wish to call Bethany Montgomery."

Ms. Parker stood to leave the stage. She seemed uneasy on her feet and for a moment I thought she would fall. She seemed both exhausted and relieved. I was confused as to why she had invested so much energy.

Bethany Montgomery was in her forties, with short brown hair and brown eyes. She wore black cat-eye glasses and her slightly overweight figure was disguised in a bulky orange sweater and brown pleated skirt. She was the type of person who would usually go unnoticed, the type you guessed would watch mostly soap operas and reality television shows. She certainly didn't look like a witch.

She had a seat and submitted to the truth spell. She seemed less concerned than Ms. Parker about being here; in fact, she appeared a bit annoyed at the inconvenience. Mr. Levi asked the preliminary questions concerning her name and how long she had known Ms. Gillis.

"I want to draw your attention to approximately one year ago. Isn't that when you started hearing noises emanating from Ms. Gillis's house?"

"Objection. Leading," I said.

Ms. LeFay definitely gave me the evil eye this time. "Mr. Roberts, I do not want to waste further time with this. Mr. Levi can lead all he wants. The witness is bound by the truth. We are not in court. Stop interrupting; it is a waste of time and of no benefit to Ms. Gillis."

"You may answer," Mr. Levi said.

"Yes, I have noticed on a number of occasions strange noises coming from her house late at night."

"Could you describe them?"

"Sometimes they are like children screaming or animals whimpering. Once I thought I heard a baby cry."

"How often have you heard such sounds?"

"Maybe five times in all, starting a year ago. The last time was two months back."

"Nothing further."

"Mr. Roberts?" Ms. LeFay said.

"You don't like babies, do you Ms. Montgomery?" I said.

"I have two daughters," Ms. Montgomery growled angrily. "What do you mean?"

"If you heard a baby cry and did nothing, you must have a problem with babies. I assume, even if you find babies annoying, that you knocked on the door to ask Bridget what was going on."

"No, I didn't. Ms. Gillis is a very private person."

"So you called the police?"

"No."

"You at least notified the elders."

"I told Mr. Levi as soon as I was made aware of what Ms. Gillis was up to."

"So you believed Mr. Levi when he explained the charges. Then you determined what you had heard would support the claim of what you were convinced had already happened?"

"I heard the noises."

"No one else was with you when you heard these noises."

"No."

"Does Ms. Gillis have a computer, a stereo, or a television?"

"I don't know. I assume so."

"So the noises could have come from any of those sources?"

She blew out a puff of air. "Maybe."

"Nothing further," I said in a voice showing feigned disgust for the witness.

"Mr. Levi?"

"Nothing further."

"It is a good time for us to contemplate what we have heard," Ms. LeFay said. "Let us break for thirty minutes."

My questions for Ms. Montgomery were argumentative and

would not have gone over well in an actual court of law. Yet, this was no court of law. I was not going to play by rules no one else was bound by.

CHAPTER TWENTY-SIX

~~~

THE FOUR OF us walked to a gazebo maybe a hundred yards from the building. The other villagers made a point of avoiding us. I expected Bridget to compliment me for doing such a great job of discrediting the first two witnesses; however, she did not seem pleased. Wendy seemed overly optimistic, as if playing a part. She tried to hold Bridget's hand but was rebuffed. Bob, the only one in the mood for conversation, gave up quickly. As a result the half hour dragged on for what seemed like an hour. When we returned to our seats, everyone was ready to continue.

"Mr. Levi, what are your plans for the rest of the day?" Ms. LeFay asked.

"I would like to call Tim Johnson and then break for lunch."

"What of this afternoon?" Ms. LeFay asked.

"I intend to call Mr. Yoder. Then I have some additional evidence to present. Also, I'd like to lead a tour of the *Blood Thorns*."

He put additional emphasis on the words. The effect was not lost on the villagers, who greeted his announcement with gasps. There are certain crimes where the very nature of the offense puts an attorney at a disadvantage. For instance, any crime where the victim is a child, particularly sex crimes or murder. Apparently, in the witch community, Blood Thorns fit into this category, perhaps because human blood is needed to grow them.

"Very well," Ms. LeFay said. "Please proceed."

Tim Johnson, sitting in the front row, took the witness seat. He had not been in the room this morning. I assumed he'd been waiting at Mr. Levi's house or store until it was his turn. He wore jeans, a flannel shirt, and Red Wing steel-toed work boots.

"Mr. Johnson has asked not to have a truth spell cast upon him. He will swear to tell the truth over a Bible," Mr. Levi said.

"Mr. Roberts?" Ms. LeFay said.

"I don't like it," I said. "He should not be allowed to testify without a spell."

"We will not force an outsider to agree to have a spell cast upon him. I will weigh the evidence accordingly. I can assure you, Mr. Roberts, it will diminish to some degree the value of his statements. Again, it will go to the weight of his testimony, not its admissibility."

Mr. Johnson testified as to his occupation and how long he had done odd jobs for Mr. Levi and other members of the community. He also repeated the story about the woman and child he saw in the field. When asked if the woman could have been Bridget Gillis, he agreed that it could have been.

I was able to establish through cross examination that Mr. Johnson had been drinking. He also agreed that he would have seen the figure for only a moment and through the small windscreen of an older Harley. In addition he was wearing no goggles or helmet to protect his vision and to keep the air and dust out of his eyes. He further admitted that he was being paid for his time today.

I did obtain good testimony on a couple of topics. First, he admitted there could have been another person ahead of the first. He also could not identify the child in any way. It could have been anywhere from a baby to a fifth grader.

I also made a point that he had not been given a lineup of people to identify. Mr. Levi showed him a single photograph of Bridget. Mr. Levi had already decided Bridget was guilty and told Mr. Johnson as much. He also admitted he thought of Mr. Levi as a friend and that he was a particularly good customer.

When we took a break for lunch I was feeling pretty good. None of the witnesses had managed to lay a glove on Bridget. I wasn't saying we had it in the bag, but it looked pretty damn good. Mr. Levi had a tough row to hoe this afternoon, even with the Blood Thorns growing at the end of it.

We returned to Bridget's house, where she and Wendy made lunch. Bob shared my opinion that everything was going well. Yet, despite our enthusiasm, Wendy and Bridget seemed reserved.

Bridget told Wendy something she did not want us to hear, and they continued to whisper in the kitchen. Wendy was annoyed enough that she left the kitchen and sat at the table with Bob and me. A few minutes later Bridget came out with beef and turkey sandwiches, pasta salad, and broccoli.

"What is the matter?" I said. "You two seem upset."

Wendy said, "No, you are doing well, it is just—"

Bridget cut her off. "It is just Mr. Levi's reaction."

"What do you mean?" I asked. I was still full from breakfast, but I took a few bites of sandwich and helped myself to the pasta salad.

"It was clear that you completely discredited his witnesses, yet he did not care," Bridget said. "He had to know that if Mr. Johnson was not subjected to a truth spell his testimony would be largely ignored."

I swallowed and said, "So what's your point?"

"My point is that this afternoon he has something dramatic planned, something that can't be good."

"We know he intends to call the Amish couple. Still, he probably doesn't know the substance of their testimony. They are unable to speak of it because of some spell. In addition, he intends to take the elders to the Blood Thorns. I have been there twice and your name is not carved into the mud."

"I know Mr. Levi," she insisted. "He has something planned. Either he knows more than he says he does about that Amish couple or he has something else up his well-tailored sleeve."

"He said you knew each other, that you were engaged to be married once. Is that true?" I asked.

"Yes, once, long ago. You need not be jealous," Bridget said.

I pushed my plate away. "It is not about jealousy," I said, "it is about his motivation in prosecuting you. It is also about your motivation in not telling me about your relationship. There is something there. I just hope it is not something I need to know. I get the feeling you two are the most powerful magical forces in this village and that this whole trial is personal."

"I thought you were skeptical of fortune tellers," she said with a bitter little laugh. "Now you think you are one. You actually do have some ability … a hint of premonitions, minor intuition. There is a grain of magic in your blood. Yet, you are still an ant trying to explain how a skyscraper is constructed. Mr. Levi and I are at a level you cannot comprehend."

"I get it," I said, trying to keep the anger out of my voice. "You want Bob and me here to make you look less dangerous, less imposing. You don't want to look dangerous and powerful— you want to look weak and innocent—so why not get an ant to represent you? To be your face in court. When this is over, do you intend to squash me? Perhaps keep me as a pet?"

"That is not what she means," Wendy said. "She needs you. Bridget is just upset."

"Yes, Wendy is right," Bridget said, starting to tear up. "I'm sorry. It is just that the accusations are so horrible, and my life is on the line. I am not myself." She pulled a handkerchief out of her pocket and blew her nose.

We ate in relative silence. After we were done Bob and I left the house and headed for the makeshift courtroom, leaving Bridget and Wendy to return at their own pace. Bob was clearly bothered by something, as was I.

Bob stopped in the middle of the field near one of the gazebos. "No one is telling us the whole truth here," he said.

I stopped, too. "I agree."

"Who can we trust?"

I looked around. At the moment the streets were deserted. "No one who is not a witch or warlock could benefit from the fruit of the Blood Thorns," I said. "Thus, if Bridget is innocent, someone else here is guilty. That person could be Mr. Levi, but it could also be anyone."

Bob scuffed the dirt with one foot. We were both restless and off balance. "That does make it tough," he said. "There are at least fifty people in this village."

"Mr. Levi is a more likely candidate than most," I said. "He collects spell books and so is always looking for more knowledge and thus more power. In addition, he was the one who first discovered the Blood Thorns."

"I see; the old passing gas theory of law," Bob said.

"I'm confused."

"Whoever smelt it dealt it. Whoever made the initial find did the crime."

"You have the maturity of a teenager," I said impatiently.

"Wow," he said, scowling, "when did you become Mr. Maturity?"

I didn't want to get into it with Bob. We weren't really irritated with each other, just the situation.

"If it's not Mr. Levi, it has to be one of the elders," I said. "It is a complicated spell and involved spilling blood. I can't see many of these villagers as being capable of carrying it off."

"That's a guess, of course," Bob said.

"Of course," I said, "but Bridget said I had a hint of premonitions and insight."

"Do you still love her?"

I couldn't look him in the eye. "I don't know," I admitted.

"You have to know that she will never see you as an equal," he said. "She may be willing to use you but she will never truly love you. There is no mutual respect."

"I know you're right, but at the same time I still feel drawn to her."

"Perhaps you are drawn to her like a moth to flame."

"This is no time for this," I said. "Whether or not we have a future, she does not deserve to die."

"Even if she has murdered innocent children and drained their blood?"

"Yes, even then."

"You've had to kill people in the past," Bob said. "I don't get it."

Bob was staring at me, waiting for my answer. "Every day I feel the weight of the souls I have dispatched," I said, meeting his puzzled gaze. "I don't want the government or even an elder of a village to have the right to kill another human being. When I killed I acted in the moment to defend our lives. The government acts with pre-meditation."

"Shit," Bob said, "you always act like I'm some kind of pacifist hippie. Yet, if I was convinced she killed a child to perform a spell I wouldn't hesitate to put a bullet in her head."

"That is you as an individual," I said. "I have seen innocent people convicted of crimes. How many times have people been released from death row based on DNA evidence? I believe our system of justice is the greatest in the world, yet we still get it wrong. Our system is only as reliable as the people who testify and the interpretation of that evidence by members of the jury. People are not machines; they are swayed by passion and prejudice. Witnesses are swayed by their own self interests. I don't trust the government to issue me a driver's license in an efficient manner. Why the hell would you give them the power to choose between life and death?" I knew I was on my soapbox and my voice was getting too loud. I consciously dialed it down a notch so we wouldn't attract the attention of the whole village.

Bob sensed my thoughts and lowered his voice to say, "What if you witnessed Bridget killing a child?"

I matched his tone. "I would blow her head off. I have to say your attitude surprises me."

"Why?" Bob asked.

"You're the one who doesn't trust cops. You're the one who buys into every type of conspiracy. Hell, you still believe aliens are being held in Area 51. Why would you trust the government or this village to decide who dies?"

"I guess I figure people would be more careful in charging and prosecuting murder cases and as a result get it right."

"I think the opposite is true," I said. "Joseph Goebbels said, 'If you tell a lie big enough and keep repeating it, people will eventually come to believe it.' It is the emotional cases like crimes against children, sex crimes, and murder where I have the least faith in the verdicts."

We walked the rest of the way to the village congregation building and returned to our spots on the stage. A few moments later Wendy and Bridget joined us. Mr. Levi had set up a large screen near the back wall next to the elders. Over the next ten minutes the room began to fill.

Ms. LeFay struck the crystal on the table and it lit up bright green. The people in the room fell silent. She looked over at Mr. Levi.

"Are you ready to begin?"

"Yes," Mr. Levi said.

"Mr. Roberts?"

"Yes," I said.

CHAPTER TWENTY-SEVEN

~~~

M R. LEVI REMOVED a small projector from a briefcase and attached an iPhone to it. He then moved the screen to an angle where the elders and the audience could best see it. Our view, however, was obstructed. I got up and moved my seat to the middle of the stage so I could see the entire screen.

Facing the elders, I asked Mr. Levi, "What is this all about?"

"I want to show the elders the pages from the journal of Hazel Waterhouse," Mr. Levi said.

"No," I said, "you want to show this entire room the pages. Why not just give a copy of the pages to the trier of fact?"

"Don't tell me how to try my case," Mr. Levi said, snarling and turning red in the face.

"I am not," I said coolly. "If I was to tell you how to try a case, I would tell you not to waste our time with irrelevant evidence. Who cares what a friend of a relative of Ms. Gillis said?"

"It shows she knows how to grow Blood Thorns," he said.

"It shows that a distant relative and friend of hers over a hundred years ago knew how to grow Blood Thorns. However, it is more a description than a recipe and does not really show anything. If you want to show what Bridget knew, you have to show she read these pages. You also need to show she did so a year ago. You also have to show the spell is sufficiently detailed to allow the reader to replicate it. Not that the hearsay of a dead woman from over a hundred years ago is relevant to this case at all," I added.

"Mr. Levi and Mr. Roberts, I have had enough," Ms. LeFay said. "Mr. Levi, give me a hard copy of what you want us to see. There is no reason to put it up on the big screen. I assume you have no objections since you suggested this, Mr. Roberts?"

"No," I said. "I can't exactly cross-examine a dead witness or attack the authenticity of the document without an expert."

"Mr. Levi, I assume this document is authentic," Ms. LeFay said.

"I swear it," Mr. Levi said.

"May I ask where you obtained it?" I said.

"If it is authentic, that is enough," Ms. LeFay said. "Next witness, Mr. Levi."

"I would ask to call Mr. Joseph Yoder."

Mr. Yoder, whom I recognized from our earlier encounters, was admitted through the back door and shown to the witness chair. He wore blue pants and a denim shirt with suspenders and a straw hat.

"Joseph Yoder, are you willing to tell us what happened to two of your children?" Mr. Levi asked.

Tears were streaming down the man's face. He began nodding and trying to speak but only grunts came out of his mouth.

"Mr. Yoder," Ms. LeFay said, "we cannot remove the spell cast upon you. Only the witch or warlock who cast the spell can do that. We can, with your consent, create a wall to temporarily block its influence, if you wish to allow it."

Mr. Yoder nodded his acquiescence. The three elders got up from their chairs. Agnes Moore removed five clear crystals from a velvet bag and placed them around Mr. Yoder. Abraham Mage took a red powder to create lines connecting the crystals to form a pentagram while Glenda LeFay walked around Mr. Yoder chanting in an unfamiliar language. When they were done I imagined—for a brief moment—a translucent wall made of water around Mr. Yoder; then it was gone. The elders moved with such fluidity and precision, they must have practiced this spell often.

"Mr. Yoder, can you speak freely?" Ms. LeFay asked.

"Yes," Mr. Yoder said.

"What can you tell us?" Ms. LeFay asked.

"I married late in life," Mr. Yoder said. "I was in my late thirties when my son was born. My eldest daughter was four and my infant daughter was born a little more than a year ago. I felt greatly blessed. I never had trouble with your lot before all this."

"Has that changed?" Mr. Levi asked.

"Yes, now that I know what you are. Satan knows what you are. The Lord certainly knows. We stayed away and lived a godly life. Yet that wasn't enough." He stood and turned toward the people in the room, pointing toward the congregation. "You are all going to hell."

"Sit down, Mr. Yoder, or you will be asked to leave," Ms. LeFay demanded.

"What happened?" Mr. Levi asked.

"It was cold, December or January, when it happened. We were sitting by the fire, the missus and myself. The children were asleep in their rooms. The sky was black and filled with clouds. The wife was knitting by candlelight and I was sitting on the rocking chair. We were as content as we could be."

"What happened next?" Mr. Levi asked.

"How does this work?" I asked. "Can I throw in questions as well?"

"Just let him tell his story. I trust we can all be civilized. Go on, Mr. Yoder," Ms. LeFay said.

"The door blew open and there was a woman in a long hooded black gown or robe. I couldn't see her face but her eyes glowed red. She blew into her hand and gray smoke started filling the room. I felt there was someone or something else in the room. I couldn't move or see. I could still hear, though. I could hear people walking up the stairs."

"More than one? 'People,' not a person?" I asked.

"I'm not sure. I know I heard the baby gurgle. I know my son who was … *is* six was coming down the stairs. I heard his footsteps. After a while they were gone and the wife and I could move again. Two of our children were gone. My other daughter, who is four, hasn't uttered a word since." Tears of anguish flowed into the crevices and wrinkles of his face.

"I am sorry," Ms. LeFay said.

"We went to the police a couple times but when we tried to tell what happened nothing would come out of our mouths. Also, bad things began to happen after each attempt to seek help. The dog, our cows, and then the horses died. That was followed by the crops in the spring. Our crops would get eaten by insects and decimated by disease, but the crops in the field next to them—the field owned by your lot—did just fine. I would forgive you and not tell a soul if you would bring back my children," he said, wiping his eyes.

"You never saw the face of the person who did this," I said. "You can't be sure it was even a woman, can you?"

"I didn't see the face. I got the feeling it was a woman, though. Maybe because she had long hair."

"Could it have been that woman?" Levi said, pointing at Bridget.

"Bridget, stand," Ms. LeFay demanded.

Bridget stood and Mr. Yoder stared at her. There was no recognition on his face but he didn't seem to dismiss the idea, either.

After a while, he said, "I don't know. It could have been, but I can't be sure."

"We are sorry. If you don't mind, we will bring in your wife as well," Ms. LeFay said. "Ask the same of her." She sounded quite sympathetic.

"I do mind," he said. "She can't take anymore. Her mind has

not been right since all this began and I don't think it ever will be. Spells are not keeping her from talking; she just can't. You all have taken my children, my animals, my crops and you are not taking anything or anyone else."

"Is there anything else you can tell me?" Ms. LeFay asked.

"You are all minions of evil. If I could kill every last one of you I would. Then, for the first time since my children were taken, I would be able to sleep. None of you, not one, is innocent." He pointed his finger to Ms. LeFay as he spoke.

"Thank you, Mr. Yoder," Ms. LeFay said, dismissing him. Anger did not register in her tone or on her face.

Mr. Yoder walked out of the room with a slight limp. He was utterly defeated. I suspected he would never be happy again. The room waited in silence as he made his way out.

His description of the malevolent creature who took his children was hardly detailed enough to ensure that Bridget was the perpetrator. The fact that it could have been and that the act was so terrible changed the mood in the room. I could feel a level of hatred that had not been there before.

"Do you have further witnesses?" Ms. LeFay asked.

"No," Mr. Levi said, "but I have physical evidence I want you all to see. First I want to show you the Blood Thorns."

"Very well, lead on," Ms. LeFay said.

We followed Mr. Levi through the village and into the cornfield. Mr. Levi made a point of saying that the field was owned by Bridget and was closer to her house than any other. When we got to the edge of the wooded area, we found Calvin keeping watch. He took on the role of tour guide.

Two thirds of the villagers had remained behind, not wanting to enter the wooded area. They were clearly afraid to look upon the Blood Thorns. When we arrived in the center of the wooded area, the Blood Thorns appeared ominous. I could hear a gasp from the villagers who remained.

"You are witnessing pure evil," Mr. Levi said.

"Are we done?" I asked.

"Not yet." Mr. Levi took a laser pointer from his jacket and pointed to a small white skull. "It is clearly the skull of a murdered child," he said. The pointer danced around the Blood Thorns, stopping periodically to alight upon a bone or ripped piece of clothing. Once the pointer landed upon the fruit, the branches curled upon it more vigorously until it was completely hidden.

"It is cold and I have seen enough," Ms. LeFay said.

"On more thing. Calvin, could you tell us what you found?"

"It was here," Calvin said, pointing to a tree trunk by the crater where the Blood Thorns were. "You and I found it sticking out of the wood when we discovered the Blood Thorns."

"By 'it,' what do you mean?" Ms. LeFay asked.

"The silver scythe, the one that belonged to Bridget," Calvin said.

"Hold on, I have not seen this scythe and have no idea how they can prove it belonged to Bridget," I said.

"Mr. Levi?" Ms. LeFay asked.

"It is back at the meeting place. That is to be the last piece of evidence," Mr. Levi said.

"A piece he never told me about until now. He should be barred from presenting it," I said.

"If that is true, it is rude," Ms. LeFay said. "At the same time I have to consider the evidence."

When we returned to the community center, Mr. Levi removed the ancient silver tool from his briefcase. It was small, and the curved blade was silver, less than a foot long. The handle was wood and had the patina of hundreds of years. Carved into the handle was a crescent moon and each suit of the Tarot Deck.

From the reaction of the people in the room these symbols represented Bridget and her family. It was like leaving your wallet with a driver's license in it at the scene of a burglary. If people were starting to question Bridget's guilt, then the momentum had changed. No one had seen Bridget use this tool. No one had seen her leave it in the stump. The evidence was circumstantial and not very strong, at least to me. It was clear I was in the minority.

I'd had a case like this once. A residential burglary where the only evidence against my client was his wallet and identification card left at the scene of the crime. He claimed it was a wallet stolen from him weeks before. There were no fingerprints, no witnesses, just the wallet. The jury found him guilty in less than an hour.

"Do you have any further evidence, Mr. Levi?" Ms. LeFay asked.

"None."

"You rest?"

"Yes."

"Thank you. We will begin your case at eight in the morning, Mr. Roberts. There will be no continuances and no delays. You have one day, October thirtieth. The sentence must be carried out on All Hallow's Eve."

Ms. LeFay struck the crystal against the table. We immediately headed for Bridget's house. The villagers avoided us as if we had Ebola. I felt the evidence was weak, but it was clear no one agreed with me. Yet, could anyone put someone to death based on what they had heard? I suspected the answer was yes.

CHAPTER TWENTY-EiGHT

~~

IT WAS NEAR dinnertime when we returned. Bridget walked into the kitchen to make something but I felt the need to get out of the village. This had been a long day and I had the urge to eat at a location where no one had ever heard of witches. I was even willing to eat at some chain restaurant that microwaved domestic versions of ethnic foods. Perhaps we'd go to Pearwasps or Tuesday's.

"Come on, guys," I said, "let's head into town and get dinner. I'm buying."

"Why don't you two go on?" Bridget said. "Wendy and I have a few things to talk about. Just get back by nine or so. I will be sleeping in the room off the library tonight, so if you need me for *anything* I will be there." Bridget put the slightest emphasis on the word 'anything.'

"Fine," I said. "Give us a couple hours and we will be back."

My spirits improved a bit once we'd left the village behind. It was as though a weight had been lifted from me. Champaign is not exactly a big city, but when I saw its lights in the distance, I felt as if I had left a desert island and landed in Chicago. I needed civilization to wash away the concept of witch trials and Amish farm life.

"So, what do you think?" I asked Bob. "The Bubble and

Cluck, the Purple Cat, the Blue Crayfish, or Groovy Sushi and Smoothie?"

"You pick," Bob said.

"Let's do the Groovy Sushi and Smoothie. All this village life makes me long for a modern restaurant experience."

Groovy Sushi and Smoothie was on North Prospect, surrounded by chain restaurants and large big box stores such as Target and Walmart. Despite its name, it was surprisingly upscale, with fresh sushi and Kobe beef.

The smoothies were also top notch. Each is named after a Samurai Warrior. I preferred the Aochi Shigetsuna, named after a sixteenth-century warrior and made using frozen bananas, lychee juice and ume—a type of Japanese plum. Bob ordered the Matsudaira Katamori, named after a warrior from the nineteenth century. It combined frozen berries, juice from mandarin oranges, and honeydew.

The restaurant itself was quiet and dark. Most of the lighting was produced by purple neon lights just below the ceiling molding. In addition there were a few sconces that gave off a weak orange light. A simple wooden bridge crossed the koi pond in the center of the restaurant.

As we entered, the waitress recognized us and greeted each of us with a slight bow, her hands at hip level but her fingers touching. We returned the bow and were led to a booth in the corner. She was a short Japanese woman in her twenties wearing a black kimono and a red obi. Her long black hair was tied back with a ribbon.

"You want sushi for two, one Aochi Shigetsuna, and one Matsudaira Katamori?" she said, clearly proud of herself for remembering our regular order.

"Thank you, that would be great," I said.

"Hot and sour or miso?"

Each of us ordered the hot and sour soup. After the waitress left, we sat in silence for a while. Both of us were weary of the trial and our time in the village but at the same time needed to discuss it.

"Well," I said finally, "do you think we are winning?"

"The truth?" Bob asked.

"What the hell," I said.

Bob's expression was unusually serious, almost grave. "You should be. There is nothing to tie her to anything other than that silver tool. No one can say they recognize her face. No one can tie this down to a date or time. You *should* be winning. Yet, I would bet you all the sushi in Japan they will find her guilty. I could feel it when they saw the Blood Thorns. When they saw the handle of that tool."

"I agree."

"So what's the next move?"

I didn't hesitate. "Call her as a witness. Maybe she can help."

"What can I do to help?" Bob asked.

"Nothing," I said. "As far as I'm concerned, you can go home and come back in the morning."

Bob looked relieved. "I will head back with you and make sure it's okay with Wendy and Bridget before I leave. Besides, I left my computer and van there. What about you and Bridget?"

"I don't know," I said. "Her indifference toward me during this trial and the likelihood she will be baked like a potato if we lose does not bode well for a long-term relationship."

"Yet you still think you love her."

I sighed. "I can't explain it, but I would take her place in that barbecue pit from hell, if I could."

Our food arrived, and we ate in relative silence. It was, as always, excellent. After eating, we left the restaurant in no mood to return to the village. Yet we got back onto the highway and did what we had to do even though each of us was desperate not to.

"Win or lose," Bob said, "you are doing a great job."

I said through clenched teeth, "Mr. Levi is a son of a bitch for not telling us about that sickle."

"Is it hers?" Bob asked. "Has Bridget said anything? Denied it being hers?"

"She hasn't told me anything."

"I hate to say it," he said, "but I get the feeling the witnesses all told the truth."

"Yeah, me too. If they wanted to lie, they'd have claimed they saw Bridget do something. I think they told the truth. Although anyone could have taken that blade and put it there."

Bob said, "I also got the feeling that Serena Parker and Bethany Montgomery were afraid of Bridget."

"I couldn't tell," I said. "They seemed afraid of something or someone, but it could have been the proceedings themselves or just the claim that black magic was used."

"I guess."

I took my eyes off the road for a second to look him in the eyes. "Thanks for getting involved with this shit. I know you probably had better things to do than spend your week in a village of witches."

Bob shook his head. "The sad part is I'm not so sure. I really had nothing good planned."

We drove in silence the rest of the way to Bridget's. I turned on the radio for a moment, but the band Jethro Tull was singing "Witches Promise," so I immediately shut it off. My mind wandered as I drove. I was hypnotized by the lines on the road and lost in thoughts of tomorrow. In the distance I saw a harvester like a green dragon rolling through the fields, leaving a trail of dust behind it. It was dark and the bright lights of the tractor distracted me. *It's late at night and late in the season to be getting the crops in*, I thought. If Bob hadn't spoken up, I would have missed the turn off.

As we approached the village, a deer ran into the road unseen until the last second. I hit the brakes hard, and the back of the car fishtailed until the car was blocking both lanes. I could smell the burnt rubber of my tires. The deer stopped and stared at me, its eyes glowing red in my headlights.

The doe was large. If we'd hit her we could have died, or at a minimum done serious damage to the car. The animal finished crossing the road, unaware of the harm she'd narrowly missed doing or how close she'd come to death.

"Shit, I got to my first kiss," Bob said.

"Am I missing something?" I asked.

"When my life flashed before my eyes, I got up to my first kiss."

"Was she cute?"

"As a bug's ear. I was in the seventh grade. I think we were both twelve. Her name was Suzie and she had freckles and pigtails. I should have married her."

"I'm sorry it didn't work out."

"That's okay. I think she became a Methodist pastor and moved to Texas."

"Her loss. Besides, you were spared a life in Texas."

"Austin would be cool, or Arlen."

"Austin does have a great music scene. They have a bridge full of bats as well. I think Arlen may be fictional."

"Like Los Angeles."

"You mean the music scene?"

"No, the fictional part."

"Yeah, I don't believe in L.A. either."

We continued on. I reduced my speed to below the posted limit and kept my eyes peeled for deer. By the time we arrived, my heart rate had mostly returned to normal.

CHAPTER TWENTY-NINE

~~~

I KNOCKED ON the front door but no one answered. It wasn't locked so we walked in. I assumed Bridget and Wendy must be in the kitchen and headed in that direction. As we entered the kitchen, I turned to see Bridget walking down the stairs.

I was shocked by her appearance. She wore a low-cut black satin dress with black stockings and no shoes. Her long black hair was combed straight back. The dress had no embellishments, but it was tight in all the right areas. The only jewelry she wore was the silver pentagram. Her makeup was dark and extreme. Dark purple accentuated her cheekbones and black makeup surrounded her blue eyes, mask-like.

When she reached the bottom of the stairs, I said, "Wow, you look fantastic. Are we going somewhere?"

"No," she said with a seductive smile, "but today is the twenty-ninth and I may be dead on the thirty-first. I thought I should look nice."

I gulped. I couldn't quite trust what was happening. "It will make it harder to get our work done when you're looking so desirable," I said. "We have to address your testimony. Where is Wendy, by the way?"

"I told her to go home," she said, brushing past me. "She's

been under enough stress, and I don't see much she can help with tonight."

"I made a similar suggestion to Bob," I said, pointing in his direction. "All we need to do tonight is go over your testimony. He wanted to make sure you were comfortable with that before he left."

Bridget looked at Bob for the first time. "Please, Bob, you have put your life on hold long enough. Get a good night's sleep tonight, in your own bed."

"I will get my stuff and take off," Bob said. "I am feeling a bit third wheelish anyway."

"Don't be silly," Bridget said in a monotone as she stared at me.

While Bob gathered his belongings upstairs, Bridget put hot water into a copper kettle and added a handful of herbs from a container next to the stove. A few moments later the tea was done and Bridget poured two cups, handing me one. Before I could take a sip, Bob was heading down the stairs.

" 'Night, dude," he said, not slowing down as he headed out.

"I guess we are all alone," Bridget said.

"What about your … cat?" I asked.

"You were going to say my 'pussy,' weren't you?"

"Not as far as you know."

The tea filled me with warmth. Combined with the heat radiating from Bridget the effect was almost dizzying. I walked over to Bridget and kissed her hard, breathing in her scent.

Taking my hand, she led me to the second story landing and walked ahead of me up the stairs to the third floor. She made sure her dress was high enough on her body to ensure I'd notice she wasn't wearing panties. When we got to the top of the stairs she allowed her silky dress to fall from her body. She was wearing nothing but black stockings. When we made it to the library, I was short of breath, a condition that had nothing to do with climbing two flights of stairs.

She opened the door to the bedroom, where incense

and candles were burning. She sauntered in and lay down seductively on the black satin comforter, her long black hair framing her pale white skin.

Confident and graceful, she took easy breaths as she stared up at me. My heart was thudding in my chest. I managed to rip my shirt as I was taking it off and trip on my pant leg as I fell onto the bed. I felt like Jerry Lewis trying to be Dean Martin.

I kissed her neck, feeling waves of heat emanate from her as I kissed her all over, moving down past her perfect breasts. Yet her body was not perfect. As I worked my way down I noticed for the first time the tiniest curved scar along her side. It was thin and looked as though it was made intentionally with a blade rather than being the result of an accident or injury.

"Why are you stopping, my love? I was beginning to enjoy where this was going," Bridget said with a laugh.

"I'm sorry," I said, "I guess I was allowing the world to distract me for a moment. Yet that is silly. After all, you are my world."

"Do you mean that?" she asked.

"Of course."

"Then I know how we can make it last forever."

"How?"

"I know how to prove my innocence."

"How?"

"When we stood before the Blood Thorns, Calvin pointed to the bones of the victims. If we could retrieve a skull, I could summon the spirit of the dead and demand to know how he or she died. Discover who the real killer was."

"Perhaps we should finish what we started and then discuss this," I said, feeling a chill.

She ran a long fingernail down my chest as she said, "Before we make love, I need to know you love me. I need to know you will help." Her finger swerved to the side just below my bellybutton.

"Trust me," I said.

"I do, my love, but we must first retrieve the skull."

She got up, retrieved a pair of her jeans and a T-shirt from her dresser, and walked into the library. Apparently, she wanted to switch from sexy to casual attire. I was unable to shift from sixth gear to reverse so quickly. It took me fifteen minutes to calm down enough to get dressed and join her in the library. It didn't help that my hands were shaking.

She had a ripped piece of paper with brown writing in front of her and was examining it carefully. It was easy to see that any thought of love or lust was gone from her mind.

"Raising the dead or the spirit of the dead is forbidden, a blood spell," I said.

"What are they going to do?" Bridget said, not bothering to look up. "They can only kill me once."

"What are we going to do?" I said. "The thorns are guarded, and even if they weren't, they would kill us if we got close enough to steal a skull."

"Nothing will harm you, my love," she said in a soothing voice, as if gentling a horse. "Come, we haven't much time."

We moved quickly down the stairs. Bridget took a three-legged cast-iron cauldron and placed it over a gas burner on her Viking gas range. She poured in a gallon of water and began searching her kitchen for various herbs and tossing them into the water. She then removed a large mandrake root wrapped in cloth from the back of the refrigerator and added that to the water as well.

I walked up to her, wiggled my fingers over the pot, and chanted, "Double, double, toil and trouble. Fire burn, and cauldron bubble."

"Very funny," she said. "Shakespeare was a stupid witch hater. We need to get going."

"Wait, I'm not done."

> Fillet of a fenny snake,
> In the cauldron boil and bake;

Eye of newt, and toe of frog,
Wool of bat, and tongue of dog,
Adder's fork, and blind-worm's sting,
Lizard's leg, and owlet's wing.
For a charm of powerful trouble,
Like a hell-broth boil and bubble.

She was growing more impatient by the minute. "If you're done, can we move on?" she said. "Shakespeare was racist, sexist, anti-Semitic and anti-witch."

I shrugged. "Who wasn't in the sixteenth and seventeenth century?"

In a more placating tone, she said, "That was not so long ago, my love."

I wasn't sure what had triggered my little recitation, except that I was trying to buy time. However, rational thought was simply not possible in the moment.

She grabbed a black jacket and I put on my own black leather jacket. Bridget also grabbed a long wooden walking stick from the corner of the front room where we hung our coats.

She began walking toward the field. I had not realized until now she was serious. We were on our way to retrieve a skull. I followed her across the road and into the plowed field. As we walked toward the oasis of trees, I wondered if we were being observed. The moon was bright, but clouds obscured it at the moment.

As we walked, Bridget sang to herself. It was a rhythmic tune in a language I didn't understand, but it sounded old and otherworldly. Entering the wooded area, Bridget raised her arms. In her right hand she held the wooden stick high in the air. She kept chanting, but the chant was louder than the simple song from before. The end of the staff glowed an eerie green like a glow stick. We walked toward the Blood Thorns, our path illuminated by the light of her walking stick.

"I could use the flashlight on my iPhone if it would help," I offered.

"No."

"What about Calvin?"

"We will address any problems as they come up."

I tripped and fell to the ground. Bridget continued on without me. This time I did turn on the flashlight from my phone. I looked down to see that I had fallen over a broken headstone. It read Bethany Clark, Our Darling, 1879-1885. There was a carved image of an angel in the marble. I got up and ran to catch up with Bridget. She had arrived at the edge of the crater.

She examined the area around the thorns with the light of her staff. The light rested on a small human skull, that of a child. A shiver ran down my spine, or as they say in the South, a goose walked over my grave.

"There it is," Bridget said.

"That skull looks small," I said. "How do you know it belonged to a child whose spirit is old enough to talk?"

"She is old enough," Bridget said.

"How do you know it's a she?" I said.

"Just get the skull."

"Me?"

"I need to keep the Blood Thorns at bay," Bridget said. "If they move toward you, I can cast a protection spell."

"Give me your staff. I can get it with that."

"I need the light," she said, retracting the staff. "Find a stick."

I did as I was told … I assume because I was out of my mind. I wandered around, chose the longest stick I could find, and walked around the crater to find the area closest to the skull. Then I shimmied down the edge until I got near enough to spear the skull through the empty eye-socket with the stick. I raised it high in the air and crawled up the edge of the crater until I could extend the end of the stick over the edge of the crater. Bridget walked around and removed the skull as if accepting a marshmallow I had just roasted for her at a campfire.

I pulled myself from the crater, feeling movement from behind as I maneuvered over the edge on my stomach. I was thrilled to be free of the pit. A few moments more and my skull might have shared a spot among those devoured by that thing.

Bridget was already leaving as I got up. I couldn't help but think that the skull was of greater value to her than my life. She had already crossed the road when I caught up with her.

"Hurry," she said, "we have very little time. I want to cast this spell as close to midnight as possible."

I looked at my telephone; it was eleven thirty. When I was a kid my folks were not overly strict. They told me to say no to drugs. They made me clean my room. But other than that, there were not a lot of rules. One rule they never had to teach me: never, under any circumstances, for any reason raise the dead.

It was a line I'd never considered crossing ... until now.

CHAPTER THIRTY

~~~

I WAS CHILLED to the bone by the time we arrived back at Bridget's house. She led the way into her kitchen, where the cauldron was simmering.

Without bothering with an oven mitt, she lifted the lid and dropped the skull into the pot. Then, from the kitchen cabinet, she removed a large antique box. The box was covered in dark blue leather and had gold writing embossed in the top. I had seen a similar box once. It was an English case owned by a physician and it contained a number of bone saws.

She opened the box. The case, custom made and form fitting, was lined in black satin and held a silver athame. There was also an empty space where a curved blade had once lain. She took out the knife; its wavy blade was the dull gray of unpolished silver. The handle had the images of the Tarot carved into it, along with a crescent moon. It was a match for the curved blade Mr. Levi claimed to have found near the Blood Thorns.

She took a moment to admire the blade. "The Danish silversmith Georg Jensen made this for our family. He compared dull silver to the light of the moon. I wondered if he was a warlock. He was a sculptor once; you can see it in his early work. This was made in 1910."

"What of the blade presented by Mr. Levi?"

"That blade is much older than the athame—hundreds of years older, I suspect. In fact Mr. Jensen used the older curved blade as inspiration for the athame I have here. He also had the box made. It is a work of art."

She removed a glass measuring cup from the cupboard as she spoke. She then took a cotton kitchen towel from a drawer and wet it with warm water. Pouring salt onto the granite counters, she rolled the wet towel into the salt.

"It is lovely," I agreed.

"It is sharp as well."

With a clean cut she brought the blade across her side. As the blood began to stream down her side she leaned over to allow the dark red liquid to drip into the cup. It looked like she had a quarter cup. She then took the kitchen towel, rubbed it in the salt, and held it against the wound. She recited a few words in a strange language and removed the towel. The bleeding had stopped.

After pouring the blood into the cauldron, she removed a rubber spatula from a copper container beneath the stove. The end of the stirrer was a bright color that indicated it was the type advertised by a celebrity chef. She stirred with quick, circular motions and started chanting.

I don't know what I expected, but I expected something. Nothing happened. I had a seat at the kitchen table and laid my head on my crossed arms. I was tired and confused.

After a few minutes I looked up and saw a girl sitting across from me at the table. She looked to be seven or eight. She had long blonde hair in braids, blue eyes, and glasses. She wore a blue gingham pinafore with a white shirt. She looked oddly like Dorothy in *The Wizard of Oz*.

"Who are you?" I asked.

"Cindy," she said.

"Why are you here?" I asked.

"We summoned her," Bridget said. She seemed unsteady, as if she might pass out.

"That can't be," I said. "She is solid like you or me, not some ethereal spirit."

"Touch her," Bridget said.

I reached over and touched Cindy's hand. There was no substance. My hand traveled right through her.

"Cindy, did someone take you away from your home?" I asked. "Did something happen to you?"

"Yes, I was so scared. How did you know?" Cindy was on the verge of tears. She put her hands up to cover her face.

"Can you tell me what this person looked like?" I asked.

"He talked funny and wore glasses."

"Can you tell me anything else?"

"He had a beard and was really tall. Taller than my dad," Cindy said.

"What was he wearing?"

"A shirt and pants," she said. "The pants were black … or they could have been blue. His shirt was white but I don't remember for sure."

"It sounds like Raymond," Bridget said. "Raymond Levi."

"Do you have a photograph of Mr. Levi?" I asked.

Bridget stood to gather her cellphone from the counter and began scrolling through photos. After a moment she placed the telephone in front of Cindy.

"Is that him?" Bridget asked.

Cindy nodded up and down. Tears began to stream down her face. Cindy was clearly not Amish and I wondered how many children had been fed to this creature, these Blood Thorns. Was Mr. Levi the killer? I did not like show-ups. A single photograph of a person is suggestive and not the best way to identify a perpetrator. Yet at the same time she seemed certain.

"What happened to you?" I asked.

"I was playing out back when somebody grabbed me. All I remember was seeing a big house and a scary dungeon."

Then, in an instant, she was gone. Bridget and I were seated at the table alone. Bridget seemed to ponder a moment before saying, "Hold on." She ran out of the room and out the back door.

She returned ten minutes later, placed more leaves in the cauldron, and began chanting again. In a moment Cindy had returned. Bridget walked over to her and held up her telephone. There was a photograph of Mr. Levi's home.

"Cindy, was this the place?" Bridget asked.

"Yes," Cindy said.

"What about this?" There was a photo of a metal door on the ground between two bushes—the type used for a root cellar.

"Yes, keep it away!" Cindy screamed. Her voice echoed and then was cut off. She was gone.

Bridget and I sat in stunned silence. I was wondering if what I had seen was real or some illusion. We obviously couldn't call a ghost as a witness. Although in witch court, who knows?

"What do we do now?" I asked.

"Tomorrow we lead the elders to that cellar and let them see the lair of the real killer—the real warlock responsible for the Blood Thorns," Bridget said.

"He might have cleaned up," I said. "I mean, if he were murdering children in his cellar he wouldn't leave the remains."

"Why not try?" she said. "What is there to lose?"

"How did you know where the metal door was—the entrance to the cellar?"

"Remember, our houses are almost identical. My great-great aunt built his house. I might even have the designs around here somewhere. I have a similar cellar behind my home."

"Why would Mr. Levi do such a thing?"

"Power, why else? Besides, he is a collector of rare books. More than anyone in this village he would know how to cast such a dreadful spell. Then he picked the perfect person to blame—an ideal scapegoat, me. I had a powerful aunt with a questionable past he could exploit. I have little doubt that if I am killed, my extensive and valuable book collection will wind up with Mr. Levi."

"I guess you have thought this through."

"When I told him I wouldn't marry him, he was furious. How could I marry a man I did not love? He was a horrible man, more interested in power than happiness." Tears rose to Bridget's eyes.

I held up my hands, palms up, hoping she wouldn't get too emotional. "You have me convinced," I said, "but just in case that cellar is empty, we still need to go over your testimony."

"No need," she said, "I will allow myself to be truth spelled. I will deny killing children and growing Blood Thorns."

"We should practice anyway."

"I can't," she said, paler than I'd ever seen her, "that spell took too much out of me. I must get some sleep."

"Can I join you?"

"Not tonight, my love. The blood and the magic were too much. Please, forgive me. If all goes well tomorrow we might wind up with a life together after all. We will have all the time in the world."

Bridget stood and began slowly walking up the stairs. I remained behind, contemplating a world of witches and ghosts. I spent the next few hours sitting on the porch, thinking about Cindy and the horrors she'd endured. I finally wandered up to my bedroom at around two in the morning. All snuggling aside, I didn't want to sleep alone. I was too chilled by the spirit of the dead child. She was so innocent, so afraid, and sadly, so dead.

CHAPTER THIRTY-ONE

~~~

I AWOKE TO find the fluffy alarm clock once again pawing me in the face. It appeared I had overslept again. I drowsily walked down the stairs to find the gang eating breakfast. I must have missed the memo that even Bob had become an early riser.

I gave everyone a tired greeting and returned to my room upstairs to get dressed. I made sure that the books Bridget had given me the night before and my notes were in my briefcase. I also included three legal pads and two pens. I was ready for trial.

I sat down and ate without enthusiasm. I wanted to talk with Bob about everything that had happened last night but could see there would be no opportunity. Everyone else had already finished their meal. When I was done eating, we headed out. We arrived at the community building in less than half an hour from the time the cat had woken me.

The room was full when we arrived. It was October thirtieth and the villagers were eager to see what defense I'd come up with. Could I pull a rabbit out of the hat? I supposed that witches didn't use that expression. They had real magic, not magician's tricks—no hats and rabbits.

Ms. LeFay pounded the crystal on the table and all was

quiet. She looked at me sternly, speculating as to what I had up my sleeve. I prayed to no one in particular that Bridget's plan would work.

"Mr. Roberts, do you have any evidence to present?"

"Yes, I propose a field trip. I would ask to take you to Mr. Levi's root cellar."

"What root cellar?" Mr. Levi asked. His features seemed to turn to stone before my eyes, but then, he was a tense man.

For the first time, Bridget stood up on her own. She looked at Ms. LeFay. She was pleading with her eyes.

"Glenda," she said in a low, urgent voice, "I know this is unusual, but so is putting me on trial for my life. I beseech you to allow this one indulgence."

"As you wish," Ms. LeFay said, inclining her head. "Please lead on, Ms. Gillis."

We walked over to Mr. Levi's house. In the backyard under a bush were the metal doors the spirit had identified the night before. The entrance would have been invisible if you didn't know it was there. The doors were the color of earth and concealed further by the bushes.

"I have never seen these doors in my life," Mr. Levi said.

"You can't expect anyone to believe that. You have lived in your house far longer than I have lived in mine," Bridget said.

"Ms. Gillis, you have selected an advocate. You will not address me or Mr. Levi directly," Ms. LeFay said.

Bridget walked up to the metal doors and pulled hard on one of them. The door opened soundlessly on oiled hinges. It had clearly been used recently.

The smell emanating from the cellar assured me that my fear that Mr. Levi had cleaned up the space was misguided. The smell of decomposition combined with urine and feces told me that what we would find below was anything but clean.

Ms. LeFay, obviously smelling what I did, winkled her nose. "Only the elders, Mr. Levi, Ms. Gillis, and Mr. Roberts are going to go down," she said. "I don't want the room's contents disturbed. The space is also too small for a crowd."

We used our cellphones to light a path down wooden steps. The smell was almost unbearable in close quarters. Bridget found a string that turned on an overhead light. The nightmarish sight before us was unimaginable.

There was a clean stainless steel pegboard with bone saws of various sizes and shapes and sharp knives. None of the tools had blood or rust on their blades. They were as clean as in any hospital. In the middle of the room there was also a stainless steel table like the ones used at a mortuary or hospital—also spotlessly clean.

The rest of the room, however, was filthy to the point of being nauseating. The floors were coated with feces and blood. The white walls were splattered with blood like a Satanic Jackson Pollock painting. What was truly disturbing were the parts of the children placed randomly throughout. It was not so much the entrails and organs—those could have belonged to an animal—it was the arms and legs that I found so sickening. It was like visiting an evil doll repair shop. They reminded us all that children were the victims of this madman. Carpeting the floor were strips of human flesh, held in place by dried blood, urine and shit. There was a hollowed-out baby in a bucket, cast aside with less care than one would discard a turkey carcass. I don't know how many children had been murdered. With so many remains, I was shocked not to have found more police reports concerning missing children. I wondered if the same magic used on the Amish family had also kept those parents silent.

Against one wall was a contraption made from an old washer machine. Two large rollers were attached to a handle with a steel bucket below. The converted laundry mangle had been used to squeeze the limbs of the children and capture the blood. In the tub below was dried blood and crushed bones as well as the head of a child who couldn't have been more than two. From the long hair I guessed she'd once been a girl.

Ms. LeFay made a sharp inhalation that made me to turn to look at her. She held a blood-stained leather journal in her hand. I peered over her shoulder as she opened the cover to reveal a bookplate with the engraving of an owl. Above the owl was written "Ex Libris Raymond Levi." She began to flip through it slowly. The blood-splattered pages were filled with sketches of dead children and Blood Thorns with writing along the edges. I assumed it contained detailed instructions and spells that relied upon the blood of children.

"I have seen enough," Ms. LeFay said. "We are done for now." She began trudging up the wooden stairs.

We all followed. I was relieved. I couldn't have stood much longer in that claustrophobic mortuary from hell. Everyone stood in silence after we escaped the pit.

Finally Ms. LeFay broke the silence. "We will meet at the community building in one hour. Mr. Levi, you will come with us."

Still, no one spoke. After twenty minutes or so the crowd dispersed. Bridget and Wendy left together, ignoring Bob and me.

"What the hell was down there?" Bob asked.

"Hell is a good description," I said.

I spent the next twenty minutes filling Bob in on all I had witnessed in the cellar. I included what Bridget and I had done the night before and how we knew about the cellar to begin with. Bob looked shocked and disturbed.

"I hope she is worth what you have been through," he said as he worriedly stroked his beard.

"Me too."

We walked over to the community center with twenty minutes to spare. I expected to be alone but it was mostly full of villagers. Wendy and Bridget did not return until the last possible moment. Mr. Levi never returned.

The elders returned to the room. Ms. LeFay struck the crystal on the table. The room was silent.

"Bridget Gillis, please stand. Your family began this experiment of bringing witches and warlocks together in America. You of all people have been harmed by our actions. You have our apologies. I hope over time we will earn your trust once again. You are reinstated as an elder of this community.

"Mr. Roberts and Mr. Sizemore, you have done your jobs admirably. We owe you our thanks. A horrible mistake might have been made. You will both always be welcome guests in our village. Yet, not tomorrow. We need that day to celebrate *All Hallow's Eve* as a community of witches and warlocks. We need that time and celebration to heal. Thank you all. We are done." She struck the crystal on the table.

The trial was over and we had won. As for Mr. Levi, I had no idea what was going to happen to him. I suspect it would not be to his liking. I feared for his life and his soul.

I got up to hug Bridget, but she and Wendy were already out the door. I didn't know if we had a future but I wanted to try. Bob and I waited for the crowd to dissipate and then headed for Bridget's house.

When we arrived, we entered without knocking. We had won. Tonight, we needed to celebrate. I hoped Bridget might even show some appreciation in the boudoir. Bridget was sitting in the front room with Wendy.

"Bridget, you are free!" I said. "It is time to celebrate." My enthusiasm felt a little forced, since she had not exactly hailed me as her savior.

Bridget looked up at me with a tear in her eye. We have won, but at what cost? Alice is dead. Those children are dead. Mr. Levi may have been evil but we were close once. There is no reason to celebrate."

"I understand," I said, feeling foolish. "I hope we can still spend the night together." I already knew the answer but I had nothing more to lose.

She shook her head and wiped the tear away from her cheek. "I owe you my life, but you are a reminder of this ordeal. I need more time."

"How much time?" I asked.

"I will call you. Please don't call me. I am sorry; I do care for you."

"You don't love me, though, do you?" It hurt to say it aloud, but better to pull the Band Aid off quickly.

"No."

"I will get my stuff."

I headed up the stairs, followed by Bob. I put my briefcase and clothes in the hallway along with Bob's belongings. Then I stopped. There was something bothering me but I didn't know what. I did know the answer might be in the library. I ran up to the third floor.

"Where are you going?" Bob asked.

"I want to take some phone pictures of the library."

"Why?"

"I'm not sure."

"Cool."

We walked up to the library. I took a number of photographs of the naked painting of Bridget's great-great aunt. I also took a number of pictures of random sections of books.

Bob and I left the house without saying goodbye to our hosts. I felt like tissue paper, used and tossed aside. I would survive and be stronger as a result.

Who was I kidding? I would probably never be happy again.

CHAPTER THIRTY-TWO

～～

B OB AND I got in our separate vehicles and headed home. When I arrived at my house, Bob's van was parked in front and he was sitting on the porch in front of the door. I got out of the car and walked up to him.

"What up bro? Long time no see," I said.

"Shit, dude, you looked like you needed some commiserating," Bob said.

"Thanks." I sat next to him on the porch.

He bumped my arm with his fist. "What a witch, huh? With a capital B."

I stood up. "Come on in. I'll get you a beer."

We walked into the house and Bob started flipping through the channels with the remote while I grabbed a couple of beers from the refrigerator. Back to normal, kind of. It was nice using a kitchen that had never contained human body parts. Even Bridget's kitchen had a skull in it. I returned with two Leinenkugels and handed one to Bob.

"Thanks," Bob said, muting the volume.

"Damn, I feel stupid and used," I said.

"I can see that," Bob said. "I'm sorry I ever introduced you."

I took a long drink of beer. Then I said, "I also feel like we are missing something, something important."

"Like what?" Bob asked.

"Like who killed Alice. Like why would Mr. Levi set up Bridget?"

"Any clue as to the answer? Other than that Mr. Levi didn't like being turned down."

"Not yet, but maybe a few more beers will provide the answer." I gulped down about half the bottle.

"Spoken like a true college fraternity member," he said, toasting me with his bottle.

"Now you're just being mean."

"You know you were spelled," he said.

"We both were," I said. "I still can't get myself to call the cops."

"I mean, love spelled, by Bridget."

"Maybe you're right," I said. "I have dated some witches in my time but she is the worst."

"The Wicked Witch of the Midwest. I keep waiting to be attacked by flying monkeys." Bob gave me an apologetic look. "Too soon?"

"Yeah, maybe a little."

"What do you think will happen to Mr. Levi?"

"Warlock on a stick—traditional Luau pig treatment."

"That bothers you?"

"Yes."

"He murdered and tortured children."

"I'm not sure." I reached for another beer.

After three more beers I decided it was time to call it a night. I couldn't think of anything else. I was tired, and I felt used and beaten. Tomorrow was Halloween and at noon Mr. Levi would be dead. I insisted Bob spend the night since we had both been drinking.

I got into bed and closed my eyes. Tomorrow was another day.

When I opened them I was in the old cottage where I'd had my most recent conversation with Cotton Mather. He was still sitting in the same chair, smoking the same pipe.

"Good to see you, my friend. You seem concerned," Cotton Mather said.

"I think I was part of something bad. I feel used," I said.

He nodded his head. "You were, as was I. She is a powerful witch."

"How were you used?"

"Witches can control dreams. She sent me to you to help prepare her case. She needed an outsider to defend her. She felt you would come across as unbiased. Didn't Lincoln say, 'He who represents himself has a fool for a client'?"

"I don't know who said it but it is true," I said.

"In that community a friend would come off as too biased. She only had two close friends—Wendy and Alice. Neither is the lawyering type. You were perfect, but you didn't understand the community. Since she wanted to feed your ego, she didn't want to tell you how to do your job. So she used me. She felt comparing her trial to the Salem Witch Trials would be the perfect closing argument."

"Only it never got that far," I said. "The bodies of children were found in Mr. Levi's cellar. They dropped all charges against Bridget."

"That is strange. Was the cellar locked?"

"No."

"Accessible only through the house?"

"No."

"So anyone who knew about it could have used the cellar," he said.

"I guess. I see you're still a lawyer at heart."

"Even in death," he said, "but I am being rude. You need rest and relaxation. I have a lovely Port here."

On a silver tray next to him stood a crystal decanter and two small glasses. There was also a lemon and a knife. He filled a glass to the very top and handed it to me. Some of the Port fell onto the old carpet.

"Sorry about the spill," I said.

"That is why I have the lemon. It cleans wine and grape juice spills off carpets and clothing. I mix lemon juice with salt to clean brass and copper. Lemon juice has a million uses."

"You had lemons in seventeenth-century America?"

"Yes, we did, but that is not the point."

"The point?" I watched as he lit his pipe with a long wooden match.

"How can I trust what you say now?" I asked. "Isn't she still controlling both of us?"

"She is not controlling us now," Cotton said. "If she were, why would she let you question Mr. Levi's guilt? No, I think we can speak freely."

"I guess, but who can be sure? She has all the power."

Mr. Mather puffed away on his pipe. Finally he said, "Maybe you are more powerful than you realize."

I knew it was a dream, but the smoke smelled so real. I awoke. The burning smell had followed me. Bob walked in.

"Dude, I burned the eggs a bit."

Chapter Thirty-Three

~~~

"WHAT TIME IS it?" I asked.

"After eleven. Sit down, I made breakfast."

"I will be there in a second," I said. "Let me get my briefcase."

I returned a few moments later with my battered Brooks Brothers leather case. I opened it up, pleased by what I saw there. In the case was the book once owned by Bridget Bishop; I had forgotten to return it. I turned to the last page, where there was a drawing of a lemon and a knife.

"What's on your mind?" Bob said.

"A birdie in a dream," I said.

I walked over to the gas range and allowed the flames to heat the first page. There was writing on only the front of each page of the book. On the back was another book, written in invisible ink with lemon juice and a quill. A secret message. I felt like a child who has just solved the big riddle. I held it up to Bob, who looked on in amazement.

It was a detailed description of how to grow the Blood Thorns. It talked about draining the blood and feeding the creature at midnight. It had a drawing of the strange laundry mangle converted into a machine to squeeze blood from children—similar to the one we'd found in the cellar. It also revealed the greatest benefit of ingesting the fruit of the Blood

Thorns: the life force squeezed from the children was granted to the person who ate the fruit. It allowed a person to remain forever young. Yet when the years stolen began to wane, the spell had to be recast and the plant reborn. It mentioned that the fruit had to be picked and eaten at the witching hour on All Hallow's Eve.

"Where the hell is my phone?" I asked excitedly.

"How the hell should I know?" Bob replied.

I ran to my room and grabbed my iPhone. I returned to the kitchen and began flipping through the pages until I located the photograph I had taken of the painting of Bridget Bishop. Except that it was not Bridget Bishop, it was Bridget Gillis … or I should say, they were one and the same. It was not just the tiny scar in the painting along her side that convinced me, it was the look in her eyes. I knew without a shadow of a doubt it was she who grew the Blood Thorns. She knew about the cellar. She'd had these houses built, so of course she knew. That is why she'd left Europe and come to America, chased out by a community starting to notice their children disappearing. I told Bob what I believed and what it meant.

"We have less than an hour to get to the village and save Mr. Levi," I said.

"We will never make it," Bob said.

"We have to try," I said, already running to my room to get dressed.

Bob made sure to grab his gun, and he handed me the Beretta as we ran to the car. It was eleven twenty when we hit the road. It would take an hour to get to the village, even if we pushed the speed limit. We had no chance to get there on time unless the process had been delayed.

It was twelve fifteen when we arrived at the location of the village, but we couldn't find it. How could we have gotten lost? We drove around until almost one. It was too late to save Mr. Levi. I couldn't believe we hadn't been able to find our way, despite having spent so much time there.

Then I noticed a familiar landmark. I pointed to the field and the wooded area where the Blood Thorns had been. We were not lost; it was the village that was gone.

"Shit, they cast some kind of spell on the village," I said. "They didn't want the outside world to witness Mr. Levi being burned at a stake."

"If it is an illusion, we can walk into the area where it should be," Bob suggested.

"It's too late to save him. Besides, who is to say we will see him even if he is being burned to death right in front of us? It's not, however, too late to stop Bridget."

"What do you mean?"

"The witching hour is twelve. That is twelve noon or twelve midnight. Bridget would definitely choose to witness Mr. Levi's burning. My guess is she will return around midnight to harvest the fruit of the Blood Thorns. All we have to do is wait."

Bob narrowed his eyes at me. "You want to head into those woods and wait until midnight?"

"No," I said, pulling into a driveway and turning around. "First I want to stop by the house of that Amish couple. Then I want to get into something warm and get a thermos of hot coffee. If you don't mind, I think we should trade the car in for a motorcycle. I don't want to be seen."

"Why bother the Amish people?" Bob asked.

"I think they killed Alice, but I want to make sure."

It wasn't long before we arrived at the familiar white house. We pulled into the driveway and were greeted by the man who'd testified about his children's kidnapping. He was holding a shotgun. When we stopped the car and got out, he raised the gun.

"What the hell do you two want?" he yelled. "I told you not to come back!"

"You and your wife killed that woman in the shop—Alice," I said. "I want to know why."

"I don't know what you're talking about," he said, waving the gun at us. "The witches killed their own."

"No, there was a Bible verse on the chalkboard. They have their own religion. Plus, the tools were old fashioned—the type you all use. In addition you sell meat and raise animals, so you know how to butcher. Most importantly, you hate each and every person in that village. You said you wanted to kill them all."

He sneered at us each in turn. "You are real clever!" Mr. Yoder yelled. "They stole my children and I can't even go to the police. She deserved to die. They all deserve death."

"You just told me about it. Maybe the spell is broken. Why not go to the police now?"

"How do I explain why I waited a year to report the kids had going missing? How do I explain what I did to that woman in the village?"

The man's wife walked out of the house, followed by their one remaining child. The woman tried to put an arm around her husband and lead him inside but he refused to be led. The wife and child walked back into the house.

The man raised his gun and I thought we were about to be used for target practice, but instead he put it down and sat on the porch. He looked up at the sky and said a silent prayer. Then he raised the gun again and placed the barrel in his own mouth. It seemed as though I saw the blood and brains spray the white door behind him before I heard the explosion of the shot. His body fell backward onto the porch. His arms and legs were still twitching when his wife came out. It took her only a moment to put together what had happened.

"Go away before I pick up that gun and shoot you myself!" the woman screamed. "You brought this on us. Go to hell." Her face was wet with tears. The little girl followed behind her, dragging her faceless doll through her father's blood.

Shaken, we got into the car and took off. Bob called 911 and told me the ambulance and sheriff were on their way. Apparently the spell cast on us earlier only worked while we were in the village. The Amish couple might have killed Alice but they had more than paid for their sins. I suspect that the girl with the doll would never get over what she had just witnessed.

"Should we double-check that the fruit is still there before we drive back?"

"No," I said, "we need to get ready, and we will be seen if we show up now. You have night-vision binoculars, don't you?"

"Fourth generation, the best of the best. Why not just burn the Blood Thorns down, pour gas onto the branches, and send it to Valhalla? Why wait for Bridget?"

"I have to know if I'm right. I don't want to believe it is her."

"What if it is?" Bob said, putting a hand on my arm. "Can you kill her?"

"I don't know."

We arrived at Bob's about an hour later. I sat on the leather sofa while Bob wandered from room to room collecting what we would need for tonight. He was like a bumble bee buzzing from place to place, returning with different items.

"Bob, I'm going to run home, change, and shower. I will get some dinner to bring back while you figure out what we need for tonight."

"Dude," he said, "get some chocolate to hand out to the little ghosts and goblins. It is Halloween."

"What do you think a real ghost would look like?" I asked.

"Like the person did when they were alive. Just more see-through. That's an odd question."

"Yeah, I guess so."

As I drove home, I thought of the "ghost" Bridget had summoned. I remembered from one of the books what they'd said about raising the dead. A spirit is transparent. A different spell is used to raise the actual corpse. That girl would have been a skeleton. There was no skin left on her body. Cindy had not been see-through. It was a trick, a glamour of some kind. She'd been too cute, too perfect to be real. It was Bridget's concept of what I thought a sweet innocent victim would look like.

I returned home and ate a sandwich and an apple. I had not eaten since this morning and was starved. Bob's attempt at making eggs had not been successful. I showered and got dressed in a black sweatshirt and sweatpants.

I stopped at the store to buy some food. Along with my regular shopping I included four bags of fun-sized Snickers and two bags of 3 Musketeers bars. What is so 'fun' about small-sized candy bars?

I waited around until about six and then called to place an order at the Bubble and Cluck. I ordered the double Gospel Bird and an Akihito Bento Box with Maguro Nigiri and Unagi.

I then printed out a note on my computer that read, "Please Take One" on card stock. I put a large glass bowl out on the porch and poured half the candy into it. I placed the sign under the candy, for all the good it would do.

By the time I picked up the food and returned to Bob's, it was after seven. The streets were teeming with small children dressed as creatures of the night and fairy princesses. Bob opened the door before I rang the bell.

"Dude, do you have the candy?" he asked. "I had to give the first few kids cans of green beans and an apple."

I handed him the bags of candy and placed the food from the restaurant on the coffee table. We began eating, only to be interrupted by a steady stream of trick-or-treaters. There was no shortage of child-sized witches.

At around nine the urchins begging for chocolate stopped coming and Bob showed me the equipment we would need. He brought out two guns, two knives, two boxes of wooden matches, a zippo lighter, two black matte jackets with hoods and finally, two sets of night-vision binoculars. I felt we were prepared for anything.

"The saddle bags of the motorcycle have ten sealed bottles of gasoline and ripped cloth to make Molotov Cocktails. In addition, there are two and a half gallons of Roundup. That should send that weed back to hell."

Bob's motorcycle was from the forties or fifties but had been almost completely restored. It was an Indian Chief and he refused to let me drive it. The paint was matte black, making it hard to see at night. He handed me a helmet and I got on the "bitch seat."

It was dark and the streets were slick from an earlier downpour, not to mention that this was not my favorite form of transportation.

CHAPTER THiRTY-FOUR

~~~

I T WAS ALMOST eleven when we arrived. The village was still
invisible, making me think of Brigadoon, the Scottish village
that appeared only one day every hundred years. We hid the
motorcycle among the trees. The crater was still there, and the
Blood Thorns had not been disturbed. The satanic shrubbery
was mostly unchanged other than the fruit, which was now a
deep red, the color of blood. Bob and I separated, each taking
up a different spot around the crater. It took two trips to carry
all the gas and weed killer from the saddle bags. Then it was
time to wait.

I found a good hiding spot behind a stump on a flat rock.
I moved after a bit when I noticed that the flat rock was an
aging marble tombstone from the nineteenth century. After
twenty minutes I got up to stretch my legs. I walked around
for a moment but tripped and fell over something. I looked to
see what I had tripped over, using my phone as a flashlight. It
was Calvin. His skin was cold, but he was alive; I could feel his
pulse. I wondered if he was injured but I could find no signs of
trauma. I was about to call Bob when I heard noises and saw a
blue ball of flame floating in the air.

"I can smell you, Sam," Bridget said. "Did you know it would
be me or did you just decide to wait for anyone?"

Bridget was at the other end of the crater. She held up a staff that glowed blue at the end. Wendy was with her. Both were dressed in black hooded capes. I stood up to address her.

"I just took a shower," I said. "I should smell like Irish Spring soap."

"One of the side effects of a love spell," she explained. "You become tuned in to the other person in peculiar ways. Now, what do you think you know?"

"Everything," I said. "Well, maybe not *everything*, but most of it."

"Somehow I doubt that," she said. "I like you, Sam, I really do, but more as a pet. You really aren't much smarter than a poodle and less so than a cat."

I pointed at her accusingly. "Bridget Bishop—or Bridget Gillis or whatever Bridget you prefer to go by after so many centuries—I have determined that the cause of your longevity is the fruit of the Blood Thorns and the years you have stolen from the blood of innocents."

"Bravo, bravo!" Bridget said, clapping.

I continued, "As for Wendy—or should I say, Hazel Waterhouse—did it bother you to murder those innocent children? Did it bother you when I bedded the love of your life?"

"Shut up, shut up!" Hazel screamed.

"You have figured it all out," Bridget said. "I am surprised … no, more than that, impressed. I guess there is nothing left to do other than kill you."

I extended my arm in a 'stop' gesture. "I do have a few questions first. If you don't mind?"

"I will give you two questions," she said, hands on her hips. "You see, I have some harvesting to do. Please be quick about it."

"Mr. Levi, what was his role? Why set him up?"

"Mr. Levi found the book he showed you. The diary of Hazel Waterhouse. He believed I knew how to grow the

Blood Thorns. Yet he just assumed my great-great aunt passed down the secret. He did not make the connection as to who I really was. I actually went out with him and we were to be married. But I was only using him to learn everything he had discovered about me and my family. He didn't know much and was worthless as a warlock and a lover."

"So he had no part in growing the Blood Thorns?" I asked. "No part in the murder of children? Just an innocent person burned at the stake for crossing you."

"He deserved to die," she said. "He is—or should I say was—a weasel, a boil on the ass of the coven."

"Why me?" I said, throwing up my hands. "Why drag me into it?"

"I needed an advocate who was an outsider. One who appeared not to have a dog in this fight. Of course you loved me, but they didn't know that. It also helped that you were an attorney and a bit psychic. I thought I could use that. You could do some minor magic if you tried. At least as well as some of the idiots in this village."

"Where does this leave us?" I asked.

"Mr. Roberts, you have had your two questions. Now you must die."

I pulled the gun from my pocket and aimed it at Bridget. She did not flinch. Clearly she was not afraid. She pointed her staff at me.

"You love me," she said. "You can't kill me."

She began to chant. The light from the staff grew brighter. The silence of the night was broken by the sound of multiple gunshots. Bridget and Wendy fell back, striking the dirt. Smoke drifted from the end of my gun.

"You actually shot at her," Bob said.

"She deserved to die," I said.

"Afraid you missed. I got them both. Went through a whole clip," Bob said, raising his gun.

"Shall we get rid of the Blood Thorns?" I asked.

In answer to my own question, I began pouring the gas onto the plant. It began to flail its branches around like an injured octopus. Bob poured the two and a half gallons of roundup into the crater.

We were about to set fire to the plant when Bridget got to her feet. One bullet had removed part of her forehead and another had left a hole where her left eye had been. A third had ripped through her throat. Her lips did not move, but a sound seemed to emanate from her. The voice was dark, malevolent, and otherworldly.

"I will take you to hell."

"Not today," Bob said, throwing a lighter into the pit.

The Blood Thorns screamed as the fire took hold. I emptied the remaining rounds of my pistol into the woman who had once been Bridget. It was over.

Somehow we had survived once again. We took the bodies of Bridget and Wendy—or Hazel, whatever she was called—and threw them into the crater. I felt bad for Hazel. She was evil, but at the same time she'd acted out of love, even if it was the love of a wicked witch.

Calvin woke up sometime later. He did not know what had happened and was confused by the whole situation. I believe he accepted that he was spelled and was just as glad to go home.

It was after midnight and the village had somehow returned. Bob and I drove back in silence, contemplating what we had just gone through. When we got to Bob's, we were both too wired to sleep. Bob poured out small glasses of Maker's Mark for each of us. We sat in silence for a moment, sipping from our glasses.

"You still feel for her?" Bob asked.

"Yes," I admitted.

"You realize she murdered countless children," Bob said.

"We don't know how old she was. It is clear she was a couple centuries old, but she could have been much older. She could have survived famine, the Black Death, the Crusades.

Witnessing such horrors has to take a toll on one's psyche."

"She deserved to die."

"Yes."

"We stopped evil. We won."

"We stopped Bridget," I said. "Evil is still going strong. I don't know if I can keep fighting."

Bob finished off his glass. "Do we have a choice?"

"We sat in silence for a while, each contemplating the answer to that question. I wanted to walk away. I wanted to leave all of this behind. I just didn't know how to do that.

"This is good bourbon," I said.

"Yeah, not bad. Does it help?" Bob asked.

"Maybe a little. I guess time is the best cure for a broken heart."

"Bourbon and country music work for me," Bob said.

"You don't like country music," I said.

"No, but it does make me realize that self-wallowing doesn't help, and that I need to put the past behind me."

"We did make a difference," I said.

"Yes."

"Whatever we do next will also make a difference," Bob said.

"Don't speculate about the future. Hiring a fortune teller set all of this in motion. Besides, how long can our luck hold out? How bright can our futures be if we continue to battle the forces of evil? We have been damned lucky so far."

In answer, Bob poured us each another shot. We sat in silence for a long time. I thought about my past and my future. We both knew the forces of darkness would rear their ugly heads once again.

At some level, I also knew I would continue to fight the hydra of evil. I would fight the impossible fight. I suspected I would die in the process. Maybe it was my destiny to die in the battle of good versus evil. But what if I could change my destiny?

Bridget said that one's future can be changed. Yet she tried to change her own and failed.

A UTHOR AND ATTORNEY **Scott A. Lerner** resides in Champaign, Illinois. He obtained his undergraduate degree in psychology from the University of Wisconsin in Madison and went on to obtain his Juris Doctor degree from the University of Illinois in Urbana Champaign. He is currently a sole practitioner in Champaign, Illinois. The majority of his law practice focuses on the fields of criminal law and family law.

Mr. Lerner lives with his wife, their two children, and their cats Fern and Quinn. Lerner collects unusual antiques and enjoys gardening, traveling, reading fiction, and going to the movies.

Lerner's first novel and the first Samuel Roberts Thriller, *Cocaine Zombies*, won a bronze medal in the mystery/cozy/noir category of the 2013 Independent Publisher (IPPY) Awards. The second and third books in the series are *Ruler of Demons* and *The Fraternity of the Soul Eater*.

You can find Scott online at: scottlerner.camelpress.com.

NOW READ THE OTHER THREE SAMUEL ROBERTS THRILLERS!

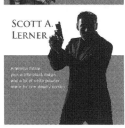

Soon after Samuel Roberts takes on the case of a man accused of selling cocaine, he is plagued by terrible nightmares. Only, when he dreams of death, people die. His investigation will involve an exotic beauty named Chloe and a synthetic cocaine combined with Voodoo herbs so addictive that its inventors have the ability to enslave mankind. Unless Sam and Bob can stop them.

Three nuns—in Chicago, Paris, and Jerusalem—have been killed in a religious ritual. Someone is following a recipe provided on an ancient text to unleash the forces of hell on earth. The final sacrifice must occur on the Winter Solstice. Once again it falls on Sam and Bob to stop the cultists before it is too late.

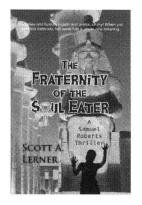

Sam seems to have a calling when it comes to stopping evil entities from destroying mankind. While investigating the case of a fraternity pledge who claims to have witnessed a human sacrifice, he and Bob uncover a nefarious plot: a group of men are combining magic and genetic engineering to bring the bloodthirsty gods of ancient Egypt back to life.